O9-ABI-879

Maigret and the Spinster

Maigret

Georges Simenon

A Helen and Kurt Wolff Book

and the *Spinster*

Translated from the French by Eileen Ellenbogen

Harcourt Brace Jovanovich
New York and London

Printed in the United States of America

Library of Congress Cataloging in Publication Data

Simenon, Georges, 1903-
Maigret and the Spinster.

"A Helen and Kurt Wolff Book."
Translation of Cécile est morte.
I. Title.
PZ3.S5892Maegwn [PQ2637.I53] 843'.9'12 76-27416

ISBN 0-15-155550-8

First American edition

B C D E

Part One

One

From the moment he lit it, in the doorway of the apartment house on Boulevard Richard-Lenoir, Maigret savored his pipe with greater enjoyment than on other mornings. The first fog of the year was an unexpected treat, like the first snow to a child, especially as this was no noxious, yellowish winter fog but, rather, a milky haze interspersed with haloes of light. The air was crisp. He felt a tingling in his fingers and the tip of his nose, and his footsteps rang out on the pavement.

A faint smell of mothballs still clung about the heavy, velvet-collared overcoat which was such a familiar sight at the Quai des Orfèvres. With his hands in his pockets and his bowler hat pulled down low over his forehead, Maigret sauntered unhurriedly toward police headquarters. Indulgently, he smiled as a slip of a girl appeared suddenly out of the fog at a run and collided with his dark, bulky figure.

"Oh! sorry, mister . . ."

She was off again in a flash, anxious not to miss her bus or subway.

The whole of Paris, that morning, seemed to be enjoying the fog every bit as much as the Chief Superintendent. Only the tugs on the Seine, invisible to the passers-by, intermittently sounded a hoarse, uneasy note.

One impression above all remained with him, though he could not have explained why. Having crossed Place de la Bastille, he was passing a little bistro on his way down Boulevard Henri IV. The door, like the door of most cafés on this cold morning, was shut for the first time for months. As he went past, someone opened it, and Maigret's nostrils were assailed by a gust of fragrance which was forever to remain with him as the very quintessence of Paris at daybreak: the fragrance of frothy coffee and hot croissants, spiced with a hint of rum. Behind the steamed-up windows he could just make out in shadowy outline some ten, fifteen, or perhaps twenty people crammed up against the zinc counter, breakfasting before rushing off to work.

It was just nine as he went through the arched gateway of police headquarters and, along with several of his colleagues, climbed the great staircase, which, as always, was thick with dust. No sooner was his head on a level with the first-floor landing than he glanced mechanically toward the glass-walled waiting room. Catching sight of Cécile sitting on one of the green velvet chairs, he frowned.

Or rather, to be perfectly honest, he deliberately assumed a grumpy expression.

"What do you know, Maigret! She's back!"

It was Cassieux, head of the Vice Squad, who had arrived close on his heels. Inevitably he would be subjected to a lot more banter of this sort, as he was every time Cécile came to see him.

He attempted to slink past without being seen. How long had she been there? She was quite capable of sitting in one spot like an effigy for hours at a time, her hands folded on her bag, her absurd green hat a little askew on top of her tightly screwed-back hair.

Needless to say, the Chief Superintendent did not escape unseen. She sprang to her feet. Her mouth opened. He could not hear her voice through the glass screen, but no doubt she had murmured with a sigh:

"At last!"

Hunching his shoulders, Maigret made a dash for his office at the end of the corridor. He was intercepted by the guard, eager to announce her. . . .

"I know. . . . I know. . . . She'll just have to wait . . ." mumbled Maigret.

Owing to the fog, he had to switch on the green-shaded light on his desk. He took off his coat and hat and glanced at the stove, reflecting that, if it was as cold as this tomorrow, he would give orders to have it lit. Then, rubbing his cold hands together, he sat down heavily, breathed a sigh of contentment, and picked up the telephone.

"Hello! . . . Is that Le Vieux Normand? Could I speak to Monsieur Janvier, please? . . . Hello! . . . Is that you, Janvier?"

In accordance with instructions, Inspector Janvier had been at his post in this little café on Rue Saint-Antoine since seven o'clock that morning. From there, seated at one of the tables, he could keep watch on the Hôtel des Arcades.

"Any developments?"

"They're all tucked up safe and sound, Chief. The woman went out half an hour ago to buy bread and butter, and a quarter pound of ground coffee. She's just got back."

"Is Lucas at his post?"

"I caught a glimpse of him at the window when I arrived."

"Good! I'm sending Jourdan to relieve you. Chilled to the bone, are you?"

"It's a bit raw. . . . But I'm O.K."

The thought of Sergeant Lucas shut up in one room for the past four days in the guise of an elderly invalid made Maigret chuckle. He was saddled with the job of keeping tabs on a gang of Poles, five or six of them, who were all holed up together in a squalid room in the squalid Hôtel des Arcades. There was nothing much to go on, except that one of them, nicknamed the Baron, had changed a bill, stolen from the Vansittart farm, at a parimutuel window at Longchamps.

This particular crowd were in the habit of wandering about Paris, aimlessly as far as anyone knew, but their lives seemed to revolve around a young woman who lived on Rue de Birague, though whether she was the mistress of one of them or was useful to them in some other capacity, no one could tell.

Lucas, disguised as a sick man muffled up in shawls, watched them from morning till night from a room in the building opposite.

Maigret got up and went across to empty his pipe into the coal bucket. He had a whole collection of pipes on his desk, and as he went to pick up another, he caught sight of the slip that Cécile had filled in. Just as he was about to read it, a bell shrilled insistently in the corridor.

The daily briefing! He scooped up the files that had been laid out for him and, in company with all the other departmental heads, made his way to the Chief Commissioner's office. They went through the usual little ceremony. The Commissioner, who had long, white hair and a Van Dyck beard, shook hands with each of them in turn.

"Have you seen her?"

Maigret played the innocent.

"Who?"

"Cécile! If I were in Madame Maigret's shoes . . ."

Poor Cécile! And yet she was still a young woman! Maigret had seen her personal papers. She was barely twenty-eight. But if ever anyone had spinster written all over her, it was she. In spite of her eagerness to be friendly, she was totally lacking in charm. Those black dresses of hers, which she made herself from cheap paper patterns . . . that absurd green hat. Beneath such wrappings, it was impossible to imagine any feminine charms. And her extreme pallor and, to cap it all, the slight cast in one eye . . .

"She squints!" asserted Chief Superintendent Cassieux.

This was an exaggeration. One could not go so far as to

say that she was cross-eyed. All the same, it had to be admitted that her left and right pupils were not in perfect alignment.

She was in the habit of turning up, resigned in advance to being kept waiting, at eight in the morning.

"May I see Chief Superintendent Maigret, please."

"I don't know if he'll be coming in this morning. I could take you to Inspector Berger, who . . ."

"No, thank you . . . I'll wait. . . ."

And she would wait, all day if need be, motionless, patient, and uncomplaining, until the Chief Superintendent reached the top of the stairs, when she would spring to her feet, seemingly in the grip of some powerful emotion.

"Take it from me, my dear fellow, she's in love."

The chief superintendents stood about idly chatting for a while, until the talk veered imperceptibly toward the work in hand.

"Any new developments in the Pélican case, Cassieux?"

"I've summoned the proprietor for questioning at ten o'clock. He's bound to talk."

"Go easy on him, won't you. He's got an influential friend in Parliament, and I don't want any trouble. . . . What news of your Poles, Maigret?"

"I'm still waiting. I intend to keep watch myself tonight. If by tomorrow there are still no developments, I'll try the effect of a personal confrontation with the woman."

A dirty bunch. Three murders in six months. All at isolated farms in the north. Coarse, brutal things, dealing death with a hatchet.

A golden glow was spreading through the fog. It was no longer necessary to have the lights on. The Chief Commissioner pulled a file toward him across his desk.

"If you have a moment to spare this morning, Maigret . . . it's a family-welfare matter. A nineteen-year-old youth, the son of a prosperous industrialist, who . . ."

"I'll see to it."

The briefing went on for another half-hour, amid the fumes of pipes and cigarettes, with periodic interruptions from the telephone.

"Very well, Monsieur le Ministre . . . Yes, indeed, Monsieur le Ministre . . ."

Outside in the vast corridors, the inspectors could be heard scurrying back and forth between the various offices, and there was much banging of doors and ringing of telephones.

Maigret, with his papers under his arm, returned to his own office, his mind occupied with the gang of Poles. Absently, he put his papers down on top of the slip filled in by Cécile. He had only just sat down when the guard knocked at the door.

"About that young woman . . ."

"Well?"

"Will you see her now?"

"Later. . . ."

First, he wanted to settle the matter in which the Chief Commissioner had enlisted his aid. He knew where to find the young man, on whom he had had his eye for some time.

"Hello! Get me the Hôtel Myosotis, on Rue Blanche."

It was a seedy hotel, where youths like the young man in question hung out to sniff cocaine and indulge their kinky vices.

"Hello! Listen, Francis . . . I think I'm going to have to close down that place of yours, for good. What? I couldn't care less. . . . Aren't you laying it on a bit thick? You can do yourself a good turn if you take my advice and send young Duchemin over to me right away. Better still, bring him along yourself. . . . I have a few words to say to that young man. . . . Oh yes, he is at your place, all right. And even if he isn't, I'm quite sure you'll know how to get hold of him before lunch. . . . I'm counting on you!"

There was a call waiting for him on another line. An embarrassed examining magistrate.

"Chief Superintendent Maigret? . . . It's about Pénicaud, Chief Superintendent. He claims that you obtained his confession by intimidation. He says you made him strip to the skin in your office, and left him there stark naked for five hours. . . ."

In the Duty Office next door, a crowd of inspectors, with their hats set jauntily on their heads and cigarettes dangling from their lips, were awaiting their orders. It was eleven o'clock before he remembered Cécile and pressed the buzzer.

"I'll see the young woman now. . . ."

The guard was back within seconds. There was no one with him.

"She's gone, Chief Superintendent."

"Ah!"

His first reaction was to shrug it off. Then, as he sat down again, he frowned. This was not like Cécile, who had once waited seven hours for him, sitting motionless in the waiting room. There were papers all over his desk. He searched through them for the slip she had filled in. At last, under young Duchemin's file, he found it.

I must see you most urgently. Something terrible happened last night.

Cécile Pardon

In response to the buzzer, the guard returned.

"Tell me, Léopold" (his name was not Léopold, but he had been so nicknamed because he cultivated a resemblance to the former King of the Belgians), "what time did she leave?"

"I don't know, Chief Superintendent. Everybody seems to be buzzing for me this morning. She was still there half an hour ago."

"Was there anyone else in the waiting room?"

"Two people for the Chief Commissioner. . . . An elderly man asking to see someone in the Department of Public Prosecution. Then . . . well, you know how it is in the mornings, people coming and going the whole time. . . . I hadn't noticed, until just now, that the young lady was no longer there."

Maigret felt a nasty little twinge of uneasiness in his chest. He was not happy about it. Poor Cécile! She wasn't all that much of a figure of fun.

"If she comes back, let me . . ."

No! He had changed his mind. He called in one of his inspectors.

"The proprietor of the Hôtel Myosotis will be here shortly with a young man of the name of Duchemin. Tell them they're to wait for me. If I'm not back by lunchtime, the hotel proprietor can go back to his work, but hold on to the young man."

When he got to the Pont Saint-Michel he was on the point of hailing a taxi, as a gesture. And precisely because he thought of it as a gesture, he changed his mind and decided to take the streetcar. The wretched Cécile and her concerns weren't all that important! Why should he concede . . . ?

The fog, far from dispersing, was thickening, though it was growing less cold. Maigret stood on the open platform, smoking his pipe. The rattling and braking of the streetcar almost shook his head off his shoulders.

How long ago was it that Cécile first put in an appearance at police headquarters? About six months. His diary was in his office, but he could check when he got back. She had lost no time in asking to see Chief Superintendent Maigret, but probably only because she had seen his name in the papers. She had seemed perfectly calm. Had she been aware that her story sounded like the product of an overfertile imagination?

By speaking, with a visible effort, in level tones, looking the Chief Superintendent straight in the eye and smiling, she had done her best to counteract the elements of fantasy in her narrative.

"I'm not an impressionable woman, Chief Superintendent, and I swear I'm telling you the literal truth. I know the exact position of every piece of furniture and ornament, as you would expect, since I do all the housework. My aunt has always been opposed to employing a maid. . . . The first time it happened, I thought I must be mistaken. But after that, I paid particular attention. And yesterday, I marked the positions of various objects. I even went further. I fixed a length of thread across the front door.

"Well, now, not only did I find that two chairs had been moved, but also that the thread had been broken. . . . So obviously someone must have been in the apartment. Whoever it was spent some time in the sitting room and, what's more, opened my aunt's desk. I'd rigged up something there, too. It's the third time in two months. My aunt has been almost wholly incapacitated for some months. No one has a key to the apartment, and yet the lock hasn't been forced. I haven't liked to mention it to Aunt Juliette, it would only worry her. All the same, I'm certain of one thing, nothing has been taken. If it had been, she would have mentioned it; she's so suspicious of everyone."

"In short," Maigret had said, summing up, "what you're saying is that some person unknown has broken into the apartment where you live with your aunt three times during the night in the past two months, and that, on each occasion, he went into the sitting room and moved the chairs around."

"And the blotter!" she reminded him.

"He moved the chairs and the blotter and searched the

desk, in spite of its being locked, and the lock's remaining intact. . . ."

"I should add that last night someone had been smoking in there!" she persisted. "Neither my aunt nor I smoke. No man came into the apartment yesterday. And yet, this morning, the sitting room smelled of tobacco."

"I'll come and have a look around."

"That's just what I wanted to avoid. My aunt isn't an easy person. She'll be angry with me, especially as I've said nothing about it to her. . . ."

"In that case, what do you want us to do?"

"I don't know. . . . I feel I can trust you. . . . Perhaps, if you could keep watch for a couple of nights in the hallway . . ."

Poor, misguided creature! Did she really think that a Chief Superintendent of the Police Judiciaire had nothing better to do than to lurk about for nights on end in a stairwell, checking up on some garbled story brought to him by a foolish girl?

"I'll send Lucas along tomorrow night."

"Can't you come yourself?"

No! Absolutely not! She was going too far! And her vexation—his colleagues were right there—was very like that of someone jilted in love.

"He may not come again tomorrow. . . . Maybe three days from now, or five or ten. . . . How should I know . . . ? I'm scared, Chief Superintendent. . . . The thought of a man . . ."

"Where do you live?"

"At Bourg-la-Reine, about a mile beyond the Porte d'Orléans, on the Route Nationale. . . . Just opposite the fifth stop. . . . It's a big, five-story brick building with shops on the ground floor, a bicycle shop and a grocer's. . . . We live on the fifth floor."

Lucas had gone there and questioned the neighbors.

On his return, he had sounded skeptical.

"An old woman, housebound for the past few months, and a niece pressed into service as part domestic, part nurse. . . ."

The local police had been informed, and had kept watch for nearly a month. No unauthorized person had been seen to enter the building at night. All the same, Cécile had returned to the Quai des Orfèvres.

"He's been in the apartment again, Chief Superintendent. This time I found traces of ink on the blotter, and I put in fresh paper only yesterday evening."

"Did you find anything missing?"

"Nothing."

Maigret had been misguided enough to tell the story to his colleagues, and soon the whole department was pulling his leg.

"Maigret has made a conquest."

The young woman with the squint, visible behind the glass wall of the waiting room, became an object of quizzical scrutiny.

Colleagues were forever knocking on his door.

"Watch out! There's someone waiting to see you!"

"Who?"

"Your lady friend."

For eight nights in succession, Lucas had lurked on the staircase and had not seen or heard anything.

"Maybe he'll come tomorrow night," Cécile had suggested.

But there was no justification for incurring further expense.

"Cécile is here."

Cécile was a celebrity. Everyone called her Cécile. Inspectors about to knock on Maigret's door would be stopped with the warning:

"Careful! He's got someone with him. . . ."

"Who?"

"Cécile!"

Maigret changed streetcars at the Porte d'Orléans. At the fifth stop, he got off. On his right a building stood all by itself, flanked on either side by waste land. The effect was of a thin slice of layer cake sticking out into the road.

There seemed to be nothing amiss. Cars sped toward Arpajon and Orléans, and there were trucks returning from the central market. The door to the building was sandwiched between a bicycle shop and a grocer's. The concierge was scraping carrots.

"Is Mademoiselle Pardon back yet?"

"Mademoiselle Cécile? . . . I don't think so. But if you care to ring the bell, Madame Boynet will let you in."

"I understood that she's bedridden."

"She is, more or less. . . . But she's had a remote-control system installed within reach of her chair. The same as I have in the lodge. And besides, if she really wants to . . ."

Five floors up. Maigret hated stairs. These were dark and carpeted in tobacco brown. The walls were dingy. Each floor had a different smell, according to what was cooking in the various kitchens. The sounds also varied. The tinkling of a piano, the squealing of children, the reverberation of voices raised in anger.

On the fifth floor, on the left, a dusty visiting card had been affixed above the bell: JEAN SIVESCHI. So it must be the apartment on the right. He rang the bell. He could hear it ringing throughout the apartment, but there was no click of a latch being released, and no one came to the door. He rang again. Embarrassment was superseded by anxiety, anxiety by remorse.

Behind him, a woman's voice asked:

"What do you want?"

He turned around to see a shapely young woman wearing an extremely becoming pale-blue dressing gown.

"Madame Boynet. . . ."

"That's her apartment all right," she replied, speaking

with a slight foreign accent. "Is there no answer? . . . That's odd. . . ."

She tried the bell herself, revealing more bare flesh as she raised her arm.

"Even if Cécile is out, her aunt . . ."

Maigret hung about on the landing for another ten minutes, then set off to look for a locksmith. The nearest one was almost a mile away. This time the sound of his approach brought out not merely the girl but her mother and sister as well.

"Has there been an accident, do you think?"

The lock, which had not been tampered with, gave easily. Maigret led the way into the apartment, which was overcrowded with old furniture and ornaments. He spared them only a cursory glance. A sitting room . . . a dining room . . . an open door and, lying on a mahogany bed, an old woman with dyed hair who . . .

"Would you please leave? Do you hear?" he shouted, turning on the three women. "If this is how you get your kicks, I'm sorry for you."

An odd sort of corpse, a fat little old woman with a painted face and stringy hair, heavily peroxided, showing white at the roots, in a red dressing gown and with one stocking, just one, on the leg that dangled over the side of the bed.

There was no possible doubt about it, she had been strangled.

Looking fierce and troubled, he returned to the landing.

"Someone go and get a police officer."

Five minutes later, he was in a telephone booth in a bistro nearby.

"Hello! This is Chief Superintendent Maigret. Who is that speaking? . . . Good! Listen, my boy, is Cécile around? I want you to slip across to the Public Prosecutor's Office. See if you can have a word with the director in person. . . . Tell him—got it?—I'm staying here. And you'd better let the forensic people know as well. . . . If by any chance Cécile turns up . . . What's the matter with you? . . . Listen, this is no laughing matter."

When he came out of the bistro, after having downed a glass of rum at the bar, a crowd of about fifty people had gathered outside the oddly shaped building.

In spite of himself, he searched the crowd for Cécile.

It was not until five o'clock that afternoon that he was to learn that Cécile was dead.

Once again, with the dining table set for two, Madame Maigret was to be kept waiting. Not that she wasn't used to it. The telephone, finally installed, had made no difference. Maigret invariably forgot to let her know. As to young Duchemin, it would be left to Cassieux to deliver the customary lecture.

Slowly, with knitted brows, the Chief Superintendent had once again climbed the five flights of stairs, oblivious of the life going on behind closed doors on every floor. He was thinking only of Cécile, unattractive Cécile, who had been the butt of so many jokes, and who was banteringly referred to by some of his colleagues as "Maigret's call girl."

This house in the suburbs had been her home. This dark staircase had been used by her every day. The smells of this place had still clung about her clothes as she sat, fearful yet uncomplaining, in the waiting room at the Quai des Orfèvres.

Whenever Maigret had condescended to grant her an interview, had there not always been more than a hint of ill-concealed irony under his mask of gravity as he asked, "Well, have the ornaments been on the move again? Did you find the inkwell at the wrong end of the table this morning? Has the paperknife escaped from its drawer?"

When he reached the fifth floor, he gave orders to the police officer to admit no one to the apartment, and pushed open the door. Then he turned back to take a good look at the doorbell. It was not an electric bell button, but a thick red-and-yellow rope. He pulled it. An old-fashioned metal bell tinkled in the sitting room.

"Will you see to it, officer, that no one touches this door."

He did not think that any useful fingerprints might be found there, but one could never be sure. He was in a sour mood. He was still haunted by the memory of Cécile sitting in "the aquarium," as the waiting room at police headquarters was familiarly called because one of its walls was entirely of glass.

It did not need a doctor to tell him that the old woman had been dead for some hours, well before the time of her niece's arrival at the Quai des Orfèvres.

Had Cécile been a witness to the murder? If so, she had not cried out, or gone for help. She had spent the rest of the night in the apartment with the corpse and, in the morning, had washed and dressed as usual. The glimpse he had had of her on arrival at headquarters had been enough to show him that she was dressed as he had always seen her.

To make doubly sure, he decided to check, as he considered it a matter of some importance. He began looking for her room. At first, he could not find it. The front of the apartment consisted of three rooms, the sitting room, the dining room, and the aunt's bedroom.

To the right of the corridor, there were a kitchen and pantry, with a door at the back. Beyond this door Maigret found a little cubbyhole, dimly lit by a skylight and furnished with an iron bedstead, a washbasin, and a wardrobe, which had been Cécile's bedroom.

The bed was unmade. There was soapy water in the washbasin and a comb on the side, with a few dark hairs between the teeth. A salmon-pink flannel dressing gown was flung over a chair.

Had Cécile known already, by the time she started getting dressed? It must have been almost as dark as night when she went out into the street, or rather into the road, for the building fronted onto the highway. She must have waited in darkness at the streetcar stop barely a hundred yards away. The fog had been thick.

On arrival at police headquarters, she had filled in a slip and sat down in the waiting room facing the black-framed wallcase with the photographs of members of the force killed on active service.

At last Maigret's head had emerged from the stairwell. She had sprung to her feet. He would grant her an interview. She would be able to unburden herself. . . .

But more than an hour had passed, and she was still waiting. The corridors were coming to life. Inspectors hurried to and fro. Doors opened and shut. People were admitted to the waiting room, and then called out one after another by the guard. She, and only she, was left waiting.

What was it that had prompted her to leave?

Mechanically, Maigret filled his pipe. He could hear voices out on the landing, the neighbors airing their views and the police officer quietly advising them to return to their own apartments.

What had become of Cécile?

During the whole of the hour that he spent alone in the apartment, this was the question that obsessed him and gave him that absent, sluggish look so familiar to his colleagues.

All the same, in his own fashion, he was working. Already, he was steeped in the atmosphere of the apartment. As soon as he had set foot in the entrance hall, or rather the long, dark hallway that served as such, he had observed that everything around him was old and shoddy. There was enough furniture in this small apartment to furnish twice the number of rooms, nothing but old furniture of no particular style or date, and not a single piece of any value. It reminded him of a provincial auction of household effects, following the death or bankruptcy of the owner, a respectable, middle-class citizen, whose austere mode of life had been a well-kept secret until then.

In contrast, however, there was not a pin out of place, and everything was scrupulously clean. Every surface, however small, was highly polished, and every ornament, however tiny, in its appointed place.

The apartment could just as appropriately have been lit by candles or gas as by electricity, so little did it reflect contemporary life, and indeed the light fixtures hanging from the ceilings were converted gas lamps.

The sitting room was more like a junk shop than a room, its walls covered with family portraits, water colors, and worthless prints in black, gilt, and fake carved-wood frames. Near the window stood an enormous mahogany desk with movable panels, of the type still to be found in the offices of the managers of big country estates. Wrapping a handkerchief around his hand, Maigret opened all the drawers in turn. Some were full of oddments such as keys, bits of sealing wax, pillboxes, a lorgnette frame, diaries going back twenty years, and yellowing receipts. Four of the drawers were empty. None had been forced.

Armchairs with worn upholstery, a shelf with knick-knacks, a work table, two Louis Seize long-cased clocks. In the dining room Maigret found another such clock. There was also one in the entrance, and, he noted with surprise, indeed almost with amusement, two more in the dead woman's bedroom.

Obviously she had had an obsession about clocks! And the odd thing was that they all worked. Maigret became aware of this fact at midday, when they all began striking one after the other.

The dining room too was overfurnished, so much so that there was barely room to move. Here, as in all the other rooms, there were heavy curtains over the windows, as if the inmates had dreaded the intrusion of daylight.

Why, when death had struck her down without warning in the middle of the night, had the woman been wearing one stocking? He looked around for the other, and found it on the bedside rug. Thick black woolen stockings. The legs were swollen and bluish in color, from which Maigret deduced that Cécile's aunt had suffered from dropsy. A walking stick which he had picked up off the floor seemed to indicate that she was not completely bedridden, but able to get around in the apartment.

Finally, hanging above the bed, was a bell rope similar to the one on the landing. He pulled it, listened, and heard the front door click open. He went to shut it, and silently cursed the neighbors who were still out there.

Why had Cécile suddenly decided to leave the Quai des Orfèvres? What could possibly have persuaded her to do so, when she had such very grave news to impart to the Chief Superintendent?

She alone knew the answer. She alone could tell, and, as time went by, Maigret grew more and more uneasy.

What could those two women possibly have found to do all day? he wondered, in spite of himself, as he looked about him, and saw furniture and more furniture laden with fragile knickknacks of spun glass and brittle china, each one uglier than the next, glass globes enclosing models of the Grotto at Lourdes and the Bay of Naples, photographs hanging crooked in cheap brass frames, a paper-thin Japanese cup with a mended handle, a number of odd tulip glasses filled with artificial flowers.

Once again, he went into the aunt's bedroom, where the body still lay on the mahogany bed, with one leg inexplicably clad in a stocking.

At about one o'clock there was a flurry of movement outside in the street, then on the stairs and on the landing. While all this was going on, the Chief Superintendent was slumped deep in an armchair in the sitting room, still wearing his coat and hat, in a haze of blue smoke from the pipe that he had been smoking continuously. The sound of voices made him start, like a man awakened from a dream.

"Well, Chief Superintendent? What's this all about, my dear fellow?"

Bideau, the Deputy Public Prosecutor, smilingly shook him by the hand. He was followed by the diminutive Examining Magistrate, Mabille, the police doctor, and a clerk who was already looking about for a table on which to spread his papers.

"Anything of interest? Good Lord! What a miserable dump. . . ."

A few seconds later, the van from the Forensic Laboratory drew up in front of the building, and the photographers swarmed in with their bulky equipment. Overawed, the police superintendent of the Bourg-la-Reine division picked his way among this impressive gathering of officials, hoping that, in due course, someone would notice him.

"Please go back to your apartments, ladies and gentlemen," repeated the policeman at the door. "There is nothing to see here. . . . Later, you will all be interviewed separately. Get out of the way, will you, please! Come along now, move!"

It was five o'clock in the afternoon. The fog had transformed itself into a fine drizzle, and the street lamps had been switched on earlier than usual. Maigret, his hat pulled down over his eyes, walked rapidly through the freezingly cold entrance hall of police headquarters and hastily went up the dimly lit staircase.

He gave a quick unthinking glance at the "aquarium," more than ever resembling a real aquarium with the lights switched on. There were four or five people waiting, in frozen attitudes, like waxworks in the Musée Grévin, and the Chief Superintendent wondered why on earth that particular shade of green, which lent a deathly pallor to the human skin, had been chosen for the wallpaper, upholstery, and table covering.

"Someone was asking for you, sir, I believe," said one of the inspectors, on his way elsewhere, with a bundle of files under his arm.

"The boss wants to see you," the guard now informed him, pausing in his work of sticking stamps on envelopes.

Maigret, without even looking into his own office, went straight on to see the Chief Commissioner. Only the desk lamp was switched on.

"Well, Maigret?"

A silence.

"A wretched business, to say the least. Any new developments at the apartment?"

Maigret sensed that the Chief had bad news for him. He waited, his heavy brows knitted.

"I did try to reach you, but you had already left Bourg-la-Reine. . . . It's about that young woman . . . a short while ago, Victor . . ."

Victor, who was afflicted with a stammer, was one of the doormen in the Palais de Justice. He had a walrus mustache and a hoarse voice not unlike a sea lion's.

"Victor was accosted in the corridor by the Public Prosecutor, who was in a prickly mood:

" 'Listen; my friend, would you say this corridor had been properly swept today?' "

Now, as everyone knew, when the Public Prosecutor addressed anyone as *friend* . . .

Maigret's thoughts were racing ahead of the Chief Commissioner's words.

"To cut a long story short, Victor, in a panic, made a dive for the broom closet. . . . Can you guess what he found there?"

"Cécile!" replied the Chief Superintendent, evincing no surprise. His head drooped.

He had had time, back there in the apartment, while

what are known as the standard procedures were being carried out around him, to consider the problem of Cécile from every possible angle, but had not been able to come to a satisfactory conclusion. It always came down to the same question:

"What could possibly have persuaded her to leave the Quai des Orfèvres, considering the very grave news she had to impart to me?"

He was becoming more and more convinced that she had not gone of her own free will. Someone had sought her out there in the very nerve center of police activity, within a few feet of Maigret's own door, and persuaded her to leave with him. . . .

What inducement had he offered? Who carried sufficient weight with the young woman to . . . ?

Now, in a flash, he understood.

"I should have known!" he groaned, striking his forehead with his clenched fist.

"What do you mean?"

"I should have known that she couldn't have left the building, that nothing would have persuaded her to leave the building. . . ."

He was furious with himself.

"She's dead, of course," he groaned, staring at the floor.

"Yes. . . . If you'd like to come with me . . ."

The Chief Commissioner pressed a buzzer and told the guard:

"If anyone asks for me or telephones, say I'll be back very shortly. . . ."

Both men were equally troubled, but the Chief Superintendent carried the additional burden of a bad conscience. And the day had started so well! He recalled the aromatic gust of hot air, a blend of frothy coffee, croissants, and rum . . . the luminous morning fog. . . .

"By the way . . . Janvier called a while ago. Apparently your Poles . . ."

With a sweep of his hand, he seemed to consign every Pole on earth to oblivion!

The Chief Commissioner led the way through a glass door. For the past ten years at least there had been talk of walling it up, but nothing had been done, because everyone found it so convenient. This was the door, in fact, which provided direct access between the Police Judiciaire headquarters and the Palais de Justice and the Archives. The building was rather like the backstage areas of a theater, full of narrow stairways and winding passages. When one was escorting a prisoner to see a judge in chambers . . .

On the right, a staircase leading to the attics which housed Police Records and the Forensic Laboratory. . . . A little farther on, a door with frosted-glass panels, beyond which lay the hurly-burly of the Palais de Justice, lawyers scurrying to and fro, the press of spectators crowding into the various courtrooms.

Beyond was another, smaller door, cut, for God knows what reason, into the supporting wall of the building itself. In front of this door an inspector was posted. He was smoking a cigarette, which he extinguished as soon as he saw the two men.

Who knew of the existence of this door? Only the personnel of the department! It opened onto a fairly deep closet, a hole about six feet square, in which Victor, who liked to have his equipment within easy reach, kept his brooms and buckets.

The inspector made himself inconspicuous. The Chief Commissioner opened the closet and, as it was not fitted with a light, struck a match.

"Here she is . . ." he said.

As there was not quite enough room for a body to lie full-length on the floor of the closet, Cécile had fallen forward against the wall with her chin pressed down onto her chest.

Maigret, suddenly feeling hot, mopped his face with his handkerchief and crammed his pipe, still smoldering, into his pocket.

There was no need for words. The two of them stood looking down at her, the Chief Commissioner and the Chief Superintendent, who mechanically removed his hat.

"Do you know what I think, Chief? Someone must have gone into the waiting room and told her I was ready to see her, but not in my own office. . . . Someone whom she took to be a member of my own staff."

The Chief Commissioner merely nodded.

"Speed was of the essence, do you see? . . . I might be ready to see her at any moment. . . . She knew who had murdered her aunt. All he had to do was to open this door, beyond which she could see nothing. Cécile had only to take one step into the dark . . .

"First, she was stunned by a blow with a truncheon or some other blunt instrument. . . ."

The foolish green hat, lying on the floor, confirmed this hypothesis. And besides, there were traces of clotted blood clinging to the young woman's dark hair.

"She must have staggered, or possibly fallen, before the aunt's murderer, to avoid making any noise, strangled her. . . ."

"Are you sure of that, Chief?" Maigret countered.

"That's what the pathologist thinks. I wanted you to be here before he started on the autopsy. You seem surprised? Why? The aunt was strangled too, wasn't she?"

"Correct."

"What are you getting at, Maigret?"

"I just don't see how both murders could have been committed by the same man. . . . When Cécile turned up here this morning, she knew who had killed her aunt."

"Do you think so?"

"If not, she would have given the alarm earlier.

According to the pathologist, her aunt was dead by two o'clock this morning. Either Cécile witnessed the murder . . . or . . ."

"What was to stop the murderer from killing her at the same time, there in the apartment at Bourg-la-Reine?"

"Maybe she was hiding somewhere. . . . As I was saying . . . or else she found her aunt's body when she got up about half-past six this morning. I know she woke about then, because her alarm was set for half-past six. She said nothing to anyone. Instead, she came straight here."

"It does seem odd. . . ."

"Not if we assume that she knew the murderer. She wanted to speak to me personally. She didn't trust the local superintendent of police at Bourg-la-Reine. The fact that she was killed to prevent her from talking proves that she knew."

"But supposing you had seen her as soon as you arrived?"

Maigret flushed, which was unusual for him.

"Yes, you've got a point there. . . . There's something I can't quite make out. . . . Maybe the murderer was tied up elsewhere before. . . . Or else he didn't yet know . . ."

With an abrupt, dismissive gesture, he grumbled:

"It doesn't make sense!"

"What doesn't make sense?"

"What I've just been saying. . . . If last night's murderer had shown his face in the aquarium . . ."

"The aquarium?"

"Sorry, Chief . . . that's the inspectors' name for the waiting room. . . . Cécile would never have gone anywhere with him, so it must have been someone else. Either someone she didn't know, or someone she knew and trusted."

And Maigret, looking stubborn and determined, stood

contemplating the sad little bundle lying crumpled against the wall among the brooms and buckets.

"It had to be someone she didn't know!" he said, with sudden decisiveness.

"Why?"

"She might have gone off with someone she knew if she'd met him in the street. . . . But not here! I confess, I was half expecting to hear that she'd been found in the Seine or on some patch of waste ground. . . . But . . ."

Bending to avoid hitting his head on the low crosspiece of the door frame, he stepped into the cupboard and struck one match and then another, and gave the body a slight push.

"What are you looking for, Maigret?"

"Her bag."

The bag was as much a part of her as the indescribable green hat. It was a capacious bag, like a small trunk, and, as she sat waiting in the aquarium, Cécile always kept it carefully cradled on her lap.

"It's disappeared . . ."

"What do you conclude from that?"

Whereupon Maigret, forgetting the disparity of rank, gave way to a burst of irritability:

"Conclude! Conclude! Are you able to draw any conclusion?"

The fair-haired inspector, who was well within earshot, averted his head. Noticing this, Maigret pulled himself up short.

"I'm sorry, Chief. But you must admit that this place is about as secure as a barn. . . . To think that someone should have been able to go into the waiting room and . . ."

He was at the end of his tether. Savagely, he bit the stem of his pipe.

"Not to mention that accursed door, which should have been boarded up years ago."

"If you had interviewed the young woman when . . ."

Poor Maigret! He was a pathetic sight, tall and heavily built, looking as solid as a rock, with his head bowed, staring at that limp bundle of clothes at his feet, that lifeless lump, and once again mopping his face with his handkerchief.

"What are we going to do?" asked the Chief Commissioner, wanting to change the subject.

Acknowledge publicly that a murder had been committed within the very precincts of police headquarters, or, to be more precise, in this breach in the party wall between police headquarters and the Palais de Justice?

"There's just one favor I'd like to ask you. Would you mind if I put Lucas in charge of that business of the Poles?"

Maybe it was just that Maigret was hungry. He had had nothing to eat since breakfast. On the other hand, he had had three little sips of brandy, which had sharpened his appetite.

"If that's what you want . . ."

"Shut this door, dear fellow, and stay on guard. I'll be back shortly."

Maigret returned to his office and, still wearing his hat and coat, telephoned Madame Maigret.

"No . . . I've no idea when I'll be home. . . . It would take too long to explain. . . . Of course not . . . I shan't be leaving Paris."

He considered ordering sandwiches, as he so often did, from the Brasserie Dauphine. But he felt he needed air. It was still drizzling outside. He decided to go to the little bar opposite the statue of Henri IV, in the middle of the Pont Neuf.

He ordered a ham sandwich.

"How are things, Chief Superintendent?"

The waiter knew Maigret. He recognized the significance of those drooping eyelids and that set face.

"Having trouble?"

A game of *belote* was in progress at a table near the bar. Other customers were playing the pinball machines.

Maigret bit into his sandwich, and thought: Cécile is dead. In spite of his heavy overcoat, it sent a shiver down his spine.

Maigret had been known to shrug when people expressed amazement at the resignation of the poor, the sick, and the handicapped, the thousands upon thousands of solitary men and women without hope, each confined to a separate little cell in the big city. He knew from experience that man could adapt to any environment, once it was filled with his own warmth and his own familiar smells and habits.

The lodge where he was now sitting, in a creaking cane armchair, was barely eight feet by ten in area. The ceiling was low. The uncurtained glass door opened onto a dark hall, for the only light on the stairs was operated by a time switch near the front door. A bed with a red eiderdown. On the table, the glutinous remains of a pig's trotter, crumbs on the brown oilcloth cover, a knife, dregs of bluish wine in a glass.

Seated opposite, Madame "Saving-Your-Presence" was speaking, her cheek practically welded to her shoulder as a result of chronic arthritis of the neck, her throat wrapped in thermogene wool, the ugly pink edge of which showed above her black shawl.

"No, Chief Superintendent. . . . Saving your presence, I won't sit in the armchair. . . . It belonged to my late husband, and, in spite of my age and all my little aches and pains, I wouldn't wish to take the liberty!"

A smell of stale cat's urine. The cat, a tom, was stretched out in front of the stove, purring. The electric light bulb, dimmed by twenty years' accumulation of dust on the shade, emitted a reddish glow. From somewhere came the sound of rain dripping into a zinc bucket, and every few seconds, the roar of a car speeding along the highway, or the rumble of a truck, or the screeching of streetcar brakes.

"As I was saying, saving your presence, the poor lady was our landlord. Juliette Boynet was her married name. And when I say 'poor lady,' Chief Superintendent, sir, it's out of respect for the dead, because she was a real bitch, God rest her soul. What's more, it was something to be grateful for, when the good Lord, a few months ago, deprived her of the use of her legs, up to a point. It's not that I want to be spiteful, but when she could get around like the rest of us, life just wasn't worth living. . . ."

When he had checked with the Bourg-la-Reine police station, Maigret had been astonished to learn that the dead woman was not yet sixty, for in spite of her crudely dyed hair, she had looked older, with her bloated face and big, bulging eyes.

Juliette Marie Jeanne Léontine Boynet née Cazenove, aged fifty-nine, born at Fontenay-le-Comte, Vendée, housewife.

With her twisted neck, her hair screwed up in a meager little bun, her black woolen shawl tightly drawn over a scrawny bosom—the very thought of the old concierge's withered breasts caused him to shudder!—Madame "Saving-Your-Presence" gloatingly savored her words as earlier she had savored her pig's trotter, pausing at intervals to direct a glance at the glass door.

"As you see, this is a quiet house. . . . At this hour everyone, or nearly everyone, is at home."

"How long has Madame Boynet been the owner of the building?"

"Since it was built, I should think. . . . Her husband was a building contractor. He built several houses in Bourg-la-Reine. He died young, he was under fifty, and it was the best thing that could have happened to him, poor man. . . . After his death, she came here to live. That was fifteen years ago. Saving your presence, she was just as bad then as she was when she died, except that she had the use of her legs and was always on my back. She was just as bad with the tenants. God help the owner if she ever caught sight of a dog or a cat on the stairs. And if ever anyone screwed up the courage to ask her to carry out any repairs . . . You'll see what I mean when I tell you that this building was the last in the whole of this area to be converted to electricity."

They could hear footsteps on the second floor, and a baby crying.

"That's Madame Bourniquel," explained Madame "Saving-Your-Presence." "Her husband is a commercial traveler. He has a small car. He's probably away at the moment, covering the southwestern territory. He's usually away for three months at a time. They have four children already, and are expecting a fifth, in spite of the fuss there's been over the baby carriage. Madame Boynet, God rest her soul, would never allow them to leave it in the lobby, so it has to be carted up- and down-stairs twice a day. There now, that's their maid taking down the garbage can."

The light went on, and a wizened woman in a white apron came into view. The huge galvanized-iron can that she was clasping to her stomach gave her a deformed appearance.

"What was I saying? . . . Oh, yes! . . . You won't say no to a glass of wine, will you, Chief Superintendent? . . . But you must! I have one good bottle left . . . a present from Monsieur Bourniquel. He's in the wine trade, you see. . . . Well, one fine day, about twelve years ago, Madame Boynet's sister, who was also a widow, died at Fontenay, and Madame Boynet sent for her three children, two girls and a boy. Everyone in the neighborhood was amazed at this generosity. In those days, she occupied the whole of the fifth floor. The boy, Monsieur Gérard, was the first to get away. He enlisted in the army, to escape from his aunt's clutches, no doubt. And then he got married. . . . He lives in Paris, somewhere near the Bastille. He hardly ever shows up here. . . . I have the impression he hasn't done too well for himself."

"Have you seen him recently?"

"Mostly he waits for his sister outside. He doesn't suffer from false pride. His wife is another one who's expecting a baby. . . . He was here last week, and went up to the apartment. He needed money, I'd think. He didn't look very happy when he came down again. The fact is, if you wanted to persuade the old lady to part with her money, saving your presence, you had to be a very early bird . . . Your very good health! . . ."

She turned around sharply and stared at the door. The light had not been switched on. Still, a faint rustling could be heard. Madame "Saving-Your-Presence" got up and swiftly opened the door. A girlish figure could be seen slinking away.

"Loitering on the staircase, as usual, Mademoiselle Nouchi! You should be ashamed of yourself."

She sat down again.

"That's the trouble with having a place this size to look after," she grumbled. "Those people! . . . They are the fifth-floor tenants, the old lady's nearest neighbors. . . . But as I was saying . . . first, Monsieur Gérard went off to join the army. Then, the younger sister, Berthe, who didn't get on with her aunt either, walked out. She's a salesgirl at the Galéries Lafayette. The old woman took the chance and rented half of the apartment space to a Hungarian family, the Siveschis. They have two daughters, Nouchi and Potsi. Potsi is the fat one, and she's most of the time loafing around half-naked. Mind you, that Nouchi, who is only sixteen, isn't much better. She goes with men at night, in any dark corner she can find, sometimes even in the entrance hall."

The best thing, he felt, was to let the concierge have her

say, and make the best sense he could of it. Thus, the second-floor tenants were named Bourniquel. The father was out of town, there were four children and a fifth expected, and they kept a maid.

The fifth-floor tenants were the Siveschis. Maigret had had his first taste of the family that morning, in the person of the fat and shameless Potsi. He had now also seen the skinny one, Nouchi.

"Their mother doesn't believe in discipline. People like them don't know about manners and dignity. Listen to this: Only last week, when I took up their mail, I knocked, as usual. Someone called out 'Come in!' . . . I opened the door in all innocence, and what did I see? Madame Siveschi, stark naked, smoking a cigarette. . . . She wasn't even embarrassed. And her daughters were there with her in the room!"

"What is Monsieur Siveschi's profession?"

"His profession! My poor dear sir, saving your presence! He comes and goes. . . . He always has books under his arm. . . . He's the one who does the household shopping. He's two quarters behind with the rent, but you won't catch him hiding from the rent collector! Rather, he seems to look on his visits as something of a joke. . . . Now, poor little Monsieur Legrand, Monsieur Gaston as I call him, he's very different. He keeps the bicycle shop. A thoroughly honorable little man, who started life selling newspapers, and pulled himself up by his bootstraps. . . . Sometimes he finds himself short at the end of the month, and, when that happens, I swear to you, he can scarcely look his neighbors in the face, not even me, although I . . . He's been married barely three months and, to save paying rent for lodgings, they sleep at the back of the shop, all among the spare wheels and tires. . . . Well, I never! I bet you that pest, Nouchi . . ."

It was Maigret who went to the door, having spotted a shadowy figure lurking outside. It was indeed the little

Hungarian, with her big, dark eyes, and her mouth like a bleeding gash.

"What do you want?" he asked.

She replied, not in the least put out:

"I wanted to see you. . . . I was told that the famous Chief Superintendent Maigret . . ."

She looked him straight in the eye. Although she was thin, with no hips to speak of, her breasts, by contrast, were well developed and pointed and accentuated by her dress, which was a size too small for her.

"Very well! Now you've seen me . . ."

"Don't I get asked any questions?"

"Have you anything to tell me?"

"Maybe. . . ."

Outraged, Madame "Saving-Your-Presence" sighed and shook her head as vigorously as her stiff neck would permit.

"Come in. . . . What's all this about?"

Nouchi skipped into the lodge as though she belonged there. She was triumphant. Maybe someone had dared her to accost the Chief Superintendent.

"I wanted to tell you about Monsieur Dandurand. . . ."

"Who's he?" Maigret asked, turning to the concierge.

And she, indignant at the intrusion of Nouchi, expostulated:

"I don't know what kind of a yarn she's going to spin you, but I can tell you, saving your presence, that those kids will lie as soon as look at you. . . . Monsieur Dandurand used to be a lawyer, a thoroughly respectable man, very sincere, quiet, and altogether . . . He occupies the whole of the fourth floor, and has done so for years. He goes out for all his meals. He never has any visitors. He'll be back any moment now, I expect. . . ."

"So what!" Nouchi stated coolly. "Monsieur Dandurand is an old pig. . . . Whenever I come down the stairs, he's watching behind his door. What's more, he's followed me into the street. Only last month, as I was passing his door, he signaled me to come in. . . ."

Madame "Saving-Your-Presence" held up her hands to the ceiling, as if to say:

"Do we have to listen to this depraved child?"

"Last Monday, I went in, just out of curiosity, and he offered to show me his photographs. . . . It was really rather revolting. He told me that if I would come and visit him sometimes, he'd give me . . ."

"Don't listen to her, Chief Superintendent."

"I swear it's the truth. I told Potsi about it the very first chance I got, and she went and had a look at the photographs, too. And he propositioned her as well."

"What inducement did he offer?"

"Same as he offered me . . . a wrist watch. He must keep a stock of them. . . . And I'll tell you something else, too. One night, when I couldn't get to sleep, I heard a noise on his landing. I got up, and went down and looked in through his keyhole, and I saw him . . ."

"Hold on," interposed Maigret, "was the staircase light on?"

She was momentarily disconcerted. He could sense her hesitation.

"No," she said at last. "But there was a moon."

"How could the moon light the stairs?"

"Through the skylight. There's a skylight just above the landing."

This was true. Maigret remembered seeing it. But, in that case, why had she hesitated when he had asked her about the staircase light?

"Thank you, mademoiselle. You may go now. Your parents will be wondering . . ."

"My parents and my sister have gone to the movies. . . ."

She looked crestfallen. Surely she hadn't expected Maigret to go up with her to the apartment!

"Don't you have any other questions to ask me?"

"No . . . Good evening."

"Is it true that Cécile is dead?"

By way of reply, he shut the door on her.

"It's a disgrace, saving your presence," sighed the concierge. "Another glass of wine, Chief Superintendent? . . . I wouldn't put it past her to be taking men up to the apartment in the absence of her parents. Did you see the way she looked at you? It quite made me blush for my own sex. . . ."

Cars and trucks rumbled endlessly past. Maigret returned to the cane armchair, which creaked under his weight. The concierge got up to refill the stove and, when she sat down again, the cat jumped up onto her lap. It was hot. Everything seemed very remote. The cars and trucks belonged to a distant world, almost, as it were, to another planet. With the lodge as the center, the real world was confined within the walls of the building. Above the bed hung the rubber bulb which released the catch of the front door.

"I take it no one could get into the house without your knowing it?"

"I don't see how, there are no keys. . . ."

"What about the shops?"

"The doors leading into the building have been bricked up. Madame Boynet was scared of burglars."

"You say that, in the past few months, she never left the house?"

"Mind you, she wasn't absolutely helpless. She was able to move about the apartment using a cane. Sometimes, she even managed to get as far as the landing, to spy on the tenants or check on whether I'd cleaned the place properly. . . . You never heard her coming. . . . She crept about in felt slippers, and she'd had her cane fitted with a rubber tip."

"Did she have many visitors?"

"None . . . except for her nephew, Monsieur Gérard, who would look in from time to time. Mademoiselle Berthe never came near her aunt. . . . I believe, saving your presence, that she has a steady boy friend. I ran into her one Sunday, when I was visiting the cemetery, in company with a very respectable-looking gentleman of about thirty. I had the feeling that he was a married man, though I couldn't see whether he was wearing a wedding ring."

"In other words, Madame Boynet lived quite alone with Cécile?"

"That poor girl! So gentle, so devoted! Her aunt treated her like a servant, but she never complained! Now there's one who couldn't be accused of running after men! And besides, she wasn't strong. Her health was far from good. She had stomach aches, but that didn't keep her from carting the garbage can down five flights of stairs, and going back carrying a bucket of coal."

"I suppose it was Cécile who took the money to the bank?"

"What bank?"

"I presume that when Madame Boynet received her rent money . . ."

"She wouldn't have put her money in the bank for all the tea in China. She was far too mistrustful. . . . Come to think of it, I remember now that, at the beginning, Monsieur Bourniquel wanted to pay by check.

" 'What's this?' she exclaimed indignantly. 'Just you go and tell the man that I want cash. . . .'

"Monsieur Bourniquel dug his toes in. He stuck to his guns for a fortnight, but in the end he had to give in. . . .

"Another glass, Chief Superintendent? I'm not a great one for drink as a rule, saving your presence, but with the right occasion . . ."

The bell sounded above the bed. She got up, leaned across the eiderdown, pressed the rubber bulb, and announced:

"That's Monsieur Deséglise, the tenant of the third-floor left. He's an inspector with the bus company. He's on shift work."

And, to prove it, a man went past the lodge wearing the cap of the municipal bus company.

"The other tenant on that floor is a piano teacher, a spinster. Her name is Mademoiselle Paucot. Her pupils arrive at hourly intervals, and you can't think how they mess up the stairs when it's raining. I'm surprised Monsieur Dandurand isn't back yet. . . . When I think of what that impudent kid dared to insinuate . . . Those little minxes, vicious as they are, wouldn't think twice about putting a man behind bars just to draw attention to themselves. Did you see the way she looked at you? You, an elderly married man and a public official. . . . I know what that means, because my husband was a public official himself. He worked on the railroad. Ah! good . . . here is Monsieur Dandurand."

She got up and once again leaned across the bed to press the rubber bulb. Lights came on in the hall and on the stairs. The soft swish of an umbrella being closed was followed by the careful scraping of shoes on a mat.

"You won't find him leaving dirty marks all over the place. . . ."

A dry cough. Slow, measured footsteps. The door of the lodge opened.

"Any mail for me, Madame Benoit?"

"Nothing tonight, saving your presence, Monsieur Dandurand."

A man of seventy, with a gray complexion and gray hair, dressed all in black, carrying a damp umbrella. As he raised his eyes to meet the Chief Superintendent's, Maigret frowned, feeling sure that he had seen him somewhere before.

And yet, when he had first heard the name Dandurand a little while ago, it had meant nothing to him. He was sure he knew the man. He searched his memory. Where could it have been?

"You are Chief Superintendent Maigret, aren't you?" said the tenant quietly, still standing in the doorway. "Would you believe it, Chief Superintendent, I've just come from your office. I know it's outside office hours, but I am also aware that occasionally you . . ."

A name leaped into Maigret's mind . . . Monsieur Charles. . . . Suddenly he was convinced that there was a connection between that name and the man who stood before him. Now what was it that that name conveyed to him? A small café patronized by . . .

"Is there something urgent you have to tell me?"

"Well . . . I thought . . . if you would be so kind as to come up to my apartment for a moment. . . . Excuse us, Madame Benoit. . . . Forgive me, Chief Superintendent, for putting you to the trouble of climbing four flights of stairs. . . . I have only just learned at the Quai des Orfèvres that poor Mademoiselle Cécile . . . I confess it was a great shock . . ."

Maigret got up and followed Monsieur Dandurand up the stairs.

"I could see you recognized me, even if you couldn't recall . . . We'd better hurry, or we'll be left in the dark. . . ."

He felt in his pocket for his key and inserted it in the lock. Maigret looked up and saw Nouchi, in shadowy outline, leaning over the banisters. No sooner had he done so than a blob of spittle landed with a plop at their feet.

Monsieur Dandurand was sensitive to cold. He was wearing a coat even thicker and heavier than Maigret's, and a long woolen muffler wound around his neck. He was unhealthy and unkempt—looking like so many elderly bachelors—and his apartment smelled as he did of stale pipe smoke, soiled underwear, and solitude.

"One moment . . . I'll switch on the light."

His study might have been that of a lawyer or a business consultant. Dark furniture, black shelves filled with law books, tables covered with green file boxes, periodicals, and documents.

"You do smoke, I think?"

He himself had a row of ten or so pipes carefully set out on his desk. Having first pulled the blind down over the window, he filled one for himself.

"Do you still not remember me? Admittedly, we only met twice, the first time at Chez Albert, on Rue Blanche . . ."

"I know, Monsieur Charles . . ."

"The other time . . ."

"In my office at the Quai des Orfèvres, eight years ago. I had a few questions to ask you. . . . And I must admit that you had an answer to everything."

A cold smile, a frozen smile on a frozen face, colorless but for a tinge of pink in the fleshy nose.

"Please take a seat. . . . I was out this morning."

"May I ask where you were?"

"Now that I know what's happened, I realize that this is going to look bad for me. . . . All the same, I may as well admit that I spend a good deal of my time in the Palais de Justice. Owing to my former connection with the law, I daresay, I can't seem to lose the habit. . . . Ever since . . ."

"Ever since you were disbarred in Fontenay-le-Comte . . ."

A vague shrug, as if to say: Just so . . . but it's of so little consequence!

And the former lawyer from the provinces went on:

"I spend most of my time at the courts . . . Take today, for instance. . . . There was a most interesting case being heard in Court Thirteen. . . . A case of blackmail within a family. . . . Maître Boniface, who represented the son-in-law. . . ."

Monsieur Dandurand, formerly Maître Dandurand, who had been living in one of the oldest private residences in Fontenay, was forever cracking his stiff finger joints.

"Please stop fidgeting with your fingers and tell me what you went to see me about in my office," sighed Maigret, relighting his pipe, which had gone out.

"I am so sorry. . . . When I left the house at eight o'clock this morning, I was unaware of what had happened in the apartment upstairs. It wasn't until four o'clock, in the Palais, that one of my friends . . ."

"You learned of the murder of Madame Juliette Boynet, née Cazenove, who, like yourself, came from Fontenay-le-Comte."

"That is so, Chief Superintendent. I came back home, but you were not here. I preferred to say nothing to the policeman on duty outside. . . . I returned by streetcar to the Quai des Orfèvres. You must have been on your way here by then. Chief Superintendent Cassieux, who knows me . . ."

"You must indeed be known, under the name of Monsieur Charles, to the head of the Vice Squad . . ."

Dandurand went on as though he had not heard:

"Chief Superintendent Cassieux told me about Cécile and about . . ."

Maigret got up and tiptoed across the tiny hallway, the door leading to which stood ajar. When, abruptly, he flung open the front door, Nouchi, whose eye had been glued to the keyhole, almost fell flat on her face. She straightened up just in time, and was off up the stairs like greased lightning.

"You were saying?"

"Knowing that I should find you here, I decided to have dinner first. . . . Then I had to wait some time for a streetcar on Place Saint-Michel. But here I am at last. . . . I wanted to tell you myself that I was in Madame Boynet's apartment last night, sometime between midnight and one o'clock. . . . She and I were friends, and I was, in a sense, her professional adviser."

Without realizing what he was doing he cracked his finger joints again, and then hastily murmured an apology:

"Forgive me. . . . Old habits die hard. . . ."

Four

It was a little after ten o'clock at night. Madame Maigret, having finished turning down the big double bed, was standing in front of the glass-fronted wardrobe beside it, putting her hair in curlers with the aid of hairpins that she was holding in her mouth. Boulevard Richard-Lenoir was deserted. The main road beyond the Porte d'Orléans was also deserted, glinting under the rain, but only a few seconds later a procession of three, four, six cars appeared on it, preceded by a broad beam of brilliant light.

These headlights, as they went past, barely brushed against Madame Boynet's house, disproportionately tall as it was, and the uglier for having no neighboring houses to conceal its rough-hewn sides.

Madame Piéchaud's grocery store was still showing a light. The proprietress was sitting in front of the stove in the shop to save fuel. On the other side of the front door of the building, the bicycle shop was dark, except for a patch of light from the open door to the back room, where there could be seen a bed and a young man polishing shoes.

The Siveschis had gone to the movies. The concierge, reluctant to go to bed while Maigret was still in the house, was consoling herself by finishing the bottle of red wine, while at the same time entertaining her cat with a commentary on the events of the day.

Over there at the Forensic Laboratory, far away on the other side of Paris, two bodies lay in drawers in that vast human cold-storage plant.

In Monsieur Dandurand's apartment, Maigret puffed at

his pipe, avoiding, as best he could, looking the former lawyer in the eye. The apartment, it seemed, was never aired, since all the usual household smells were blended in a sickening, musty staleness that seeped into one's clothing and clung for a long time afterward.

"Tell me, Monsieur Dandurand . . . if I'm not mistaken, it was in connection with a vice charge, was it not, that you were forced to leave Fontenay? Let's see . . . it's ancient history by now, but your name came up at police headquarters only a few weeks back . . . you got two years."

"That's right," the lawyer replied coolly.

And Maigret huddled deeper into his heavy overcoat, as if to insulate himself against any physical contact with this man. He had not taken off his hat. In spite of his apparent grumpiness, Maigret was very generous toward most forms of human weakness, but there were some people who so revolted him that he physically shrank from them. Monsieur Dandurand was among them.

This revulsion was so deep-seated that Maigret was never wholly at ease in the presence of his colleague Cassieux, who, as head of the Vice Squad, was in charge of all matters connected with personal morality.

It was Cassieux who had spoken to him of this man, generally known as Monsieur Charles, a lawyer from the provinces, who had been mixed up in a nasty case concerning the corruption of minors, and had served a two-year term before landing up in Paris.

His was a rather unusual case, conducive to reflections on the strangeness of human destiny. Barred from the exercise of his profession, and swallowed up in the capital city where he was unknown, Dandurand, still possessed of an ample income from investments, was able freely to gratify his vicious tastes. He was one of those dingy, somewhat repulsive, shifty-eyed men who during daytime keep in the shadows and only come to life when they are elbowing their way through the crowds in pursuit of a likely victim.

The former lawyer had been spotted loitering near the Porte Saint-Martin, Boulevard Sébastopol, and the Bastille—one of the many furtive characters that haunt factory gates and the exits of big stores, and who, at nightfall, scuffle, hunched up and muffled, into the dark doorway of some disreputable establishment catering to their special tastes.

Needless to say, he was familiar with all such establishments, and was well known to those who ran them.

"Hello, Monsieur Charles. . . . Let me see, what have I got for you today?"

He was at home in such places. They had become the breath of life to him, and he needed to go there every day. It did not take long for the other habitués to discover that he had formerly been a lawyer. He was occasionally asked to give legal advice.

By now, he had joined the chosen few who were admitted behind the scenes. He was no longer received as a client but as a friend.

"Have you heard that the house on Rue d'Antin is up for sale? Dédé has had some trouble, and he's leaving next week for South America. . . . With five hundred thousand francs to his credit. . . ."

Maigret seemed to be lost in a dream. His head lowered, he was staring at the faded red fitted carpet. Suddenly he started. He thought he had heard a sound from the floor above. For a second, he had imagined it came from Madame Boynet's apartment. The thought of Cécile . . .

"It's only Nouchi," said Monsieur Dandurand, with a characteristically mirthless smile.

Obviously, since Cécile was dead!

Cécile was dead! At that very moment, the Chief Commissioner of the Police Judiciaire, playing bridge at a friend's house, was briefly describing the scene in the broom closet, the body hunched against the wall, the tall figure of Maigret bending over it.

"What did *he* say?"

"Nothing . . . he just stood there with his hands in his pockets. . . . I think he was harder hit than at any time during his career. Then he left the building. I would be greatly surprised if he got any sleep tonight. . . . Poor old Maigret."

Maigret tapped out his pipe on the heel of his shoe, emptying the ash onto the carpet.

"Did you look after Madame Boynet's business interests?" he asked, speaking slowly with a wry mouth, as if the words had a bitter taste.

"I knew her and her sister in Fontenay-le-Comte. . . . You might almost say we were neighbors. It was only when I took a lease on this apartment that I discovered she owned the building. She was a widow by that time. . . . You never knew her when she was alive, did you? I wouldn't go so far as to say that she was mad, but she was certainly something of an eccentric. She was obsessed with money. She kept her entire fortune in the apartment, because she was terrified of being robbed by the banks."

"Very much to your advantage, I don't doubt!"

It did not take much effort of imagination for Maigret to envisage this man worming his way into the confidence of the elderly women who ran the establishments which he patronized. Later, Monsieur Dandurand had taken a step up the ladder and become acquainted with the landlords, whom he would join in a game of *belote* in the evenings in some bar in Montmartre.

Thus, Maître Charles Dandurand, lawyer from Fontenay, had been transformed into Monsieur Charles, adviser and associate of these gentlemen, who reposed great trust in him, since, being in the know as he was, he could be extremely useful to them in many ways.

"It was all to her advantage, Chief Superintendent!"

His long, bloodless, hairy hands fidgeted with the pipes on the table. His nostrils also sprouted tufts of gray hair.

"Surely you must have heard of old Juliette? It's true, you've always specialized in murder. But your colleague, Cassieux . . . It all started with the house on Rue d'Antin, which was up for sale. I mentioned it to Madame Boynet, whom I always called Juliette, since we had known one another from the time when we were young. Juliette bought it. A year later, I acquired Le Paradis in Béziers on her behalf, and that is one of the most profitable establishments of its kind in the country."

"Did she know what sort of place you were investing her money in?"

"Look, Chief Superintendent, I've known a few misers in my time . . . a lawyer in the provinces meets all sorts of people. But their greed was nothing in comparison with Juliette's. Money had a sort of mystical fascination for her. Ask anyone in the *milieu*, as you call it at police headquarters . . . ask them how many of their establishments are owned by Juliette. Allow me to quote you a few figures. . . ."

He got up and took from a wall safe a grubby ledger. As he turned over the pages, he licked his unsavory fingers.

"Last year, I remitted to Juliette five hundred and ninety thousand francs in bills . . . a profit of five hundred and ninety thousand francs."

"And she kept all that money in her apartment?"

"I have every reason to believe she did, as she had ceased to be able to go out herself and she would never have entrusted her niece with such large sums of money. . . . Oh! I can guess what you're thinking. . . . I realize that what has happened puts me in a false position. . . . But I give you my word, Chief Superintendent, that you are mistaken . . . I have never done anyone out of a single penny. Ask any of the people concerned. I don't have to tell you that they're not the sort to permit any irregularity to go unpunished. Any one of them will tell you that Monsieur Charles is on the level. . . . Would you care for a refill of tobacco?"

Maigret declined the proffered tobacco pouch and took his own out of his pocket.

"No, thanks."

"As you prefer . . . I'm doing my best to give you a truthful account. . . . As Albert would say, I am spilling the beans."

This slang expression was accompanied by an odd smile. After all, this was a man who had spent the greater part of his life in the society of the most God-fearing citizens of Fontenay.

"Juliette had a bee in her bonnet about keeping the nature of her investments secret. . . . She dreaded discovery. . . . Mark you, she never saw a soul, there was nobody to poke his nose into her affairs. All the same, she went to absurd lengths—it was almost touching—to prevent discovery. For the past six months or more, since she first became housebound, I have been under orders to visit her clandestinely in her apartment. You wouldn't believe the shifts I was put to on the days when I had to call on her. . . ."

Footsteps on the stairs. The Siveschis had returned. They could be heard talking loudly in Hungarian, and by the time they reached the floor above a regular row had broken out.

"Every morning, the tenants' newspapers are delivered to the lodge. The concierge sorts them out and puts them in the appropriate pigeonholes with the mail. . . . I had to contrive to mark Juliette's paper with a penciled cross when I collected my own. Poor Cécile, who suspected nothing, would come down and fetch her aunt's paper a few minutes later. That same night, at midnight, I would creep upstairs without making a sound. . . . Juliette would be waiting for me at the door, leaning on her cane."

The entire staff of the Police Judiciaire had openly laughed at Cécile for suggesting that furniture and ornaments had been moved during the night!

"Did the niece sleep through it all?"

"Cécile? Her aunt saw to it that she did. If you have searched the apartment, as I presume you have, you must have found several bottles of sleeping pills in a drawer. On the nights when Juliette was expecting me, she always made sure that Cécile would sleep very soundly and . . . Forgive me, I haven't offered you a drink. . . . What will you have?"

"Nothing, thank you."

"I see. . . . You're on the wrong track, Chief Superintendent. . . . Of course you don't have to believe me, but I do assure you that I couldn't so much as wring the neck of a chicken, and I turn faint at the sight of blood."

"Madame Boynet was strangled."

At this, the former lawyer seemed momentarily taken aback. He looked down at his bloodless hands.

"That, too, would be beyond me. Besides, it was not in my own interest to . . ."

"Tell me, Monsieur Dandurand, according to your calculations, how much money did Madame Boynet keep in the apartment?"

"Approximately eight hundred thousand francs."

"Do you know where this money was hidden?"

"She never told me. . . . Knowing her as I did, I presumed that she never let it out of her hands, that it must be somewhere within her reach, and that, in a manner of speaking, she went to bed with her fortune."

"And yet none of it has been found. Presumably, she also had papers, the deeds of her various properties and so on. They have vanished from her desk. What time did you return to your apartment last night?"

"Between one and half-past."

"According to the pathologist, Madame Boynet was killed at around two o'clock in the morning. The concierge states that no one entered the building. One more question: did anything occur while you were in the apartment to suggest that Cécile might not be asleep?"

"Nothing."

"Think hard. . . . *Are you absolutely sure you couldn't have left something behind in the apartment which might have made it possible for her to suspect that you had been there?*"

Monsieur Charles thought for a moment, but did not seem bothered by the question.

"I don't see . . ."

"That's all I wanted to know. Naturally, I must ask you not to leave Paris. Indeed, I should prefer it if you wouldn't leave your apartment."

"I understand."

Maigret was already at the front door.

"Sorry . . . I almost forgot . . . do your friends often visit you here?" He stressed the word "friends."

"Not one of them has ever set foot in this building. I am a careful man myself, Chief Superintendent. . . . Not excessively careful, like my friend Juliette . . . I'm not obsessional. My friends, as you call them, don't know where I live, and communicate with me through a post office box number. Still less would they be likely to know Madame Boynet's address. They don't even know her real name. In fact, a lot of people believed that Juliette didn't really exist, that she was a convenient fiction dreamed up by me for my own purposes."

More footsteps on the stairs. The voice of the concierge, out of breath:

"Just a minute, Monsieur Gérard . . ."

And she called out:

"Chief Superintendent! Chief Superintendent!"

Maigret opened the door and pressed the time switch to turn on the light, which had just gone out. A young man in a state of intense agitation, a stranger to him, stood trembling before him.

"Where is my sister?" he demanded, looking wide-eyed at Maigret.

"This is Monsieur Gérard," explained Madame Benoit. "He burst in like a madman . . . I told him that Mademoiselle Cécile . . ."

"Please return to your apartment, Monsieur Dandurand!" snapped Maigret.

The door to the Siveschis' apartment had been opened. Another door opened on the floor below.

"Come with me, Monsieur Gérard. . . . You may return to your lodge, Madame Benoit."

The Chief Superintendent had the key to the dead woman's apartment in his pocket. He ushered the young man in and bolted the door.

"Have you really only just heard?"

"Is it true? Is Cécile dead?"

"Who told you?"

"The concierge. . . ."

The apartment had been turned inside out by the technicians from the Forensic Laboratory. Drawers and cupboards had been searched, and their contents scattered all over the place.

"I want to know about my sister."

"Yes, Cécile is dead."

Gérard was in such a state of nervous tension that he was not even able to shed a tear. He looked about him in utter bewilderment, his face twitching so horribly that it was painful to watch.

"It's not possible. . . . Where is she?"

He made a dive for his sister's bedroom, but the Chief Superintendent restrained him.

"She's not here. Take it easy. Wait. . . ."

He remembered having seen a bottle of rum in a cupboard. He got it and held it out to the young man.

"Have a drink. How did you find out?"

"I was in a café when . . ."

"Forgive me . . . I'm going to ask you a few questions. It's the quickest way. . . . What were you doing this afternoon?"

"I went to three different addresses . . . I was looking for a job."

"What sort of job?"

Gérard replied with a wry smile:

"Anything I could get! My wife is expecting a baby any day now . . . Our landlord has given us notice . . . I . . ."

"Did you go back home for dinner?"

"No . . . I was in this café . . ."

It was only then that Maigret realized that Gérard, though perhaps not exactly drunk, had been drinking a little too freely.

"Were you looking for a job in this café?"

A hard, hostile stare.

"You too! . . . But, of course . . . just like my wife! . . . How can you know what it's like to chase after nonexistent jobs from morning till night? Do you know what I did last week, three nights running? No, of course not! As if you cared! Well! I unloaded vegetables at the market, just to be able to buy food. . . . Tonight, I went to the café to meet someone who had promised me a job."

"Who was that?"

"I don't know his name. . . . He's tall and redheaded, and he sells radio equipment."

"What was the name of the café?"

"Do you suspect me of killing my aunt?"

He was shaking from head to foot, and seemed on the

point of hurling himself like a madman at the Chief Superintendent.

"The Canon de la Bastille, if you really want to know. I live on Rue du Pas-de-la-Mule. My friend didn't show up. I didn't want to go back home without . . ."

"Haven't you had any dinner?"

"What's that got to do with you? . . . Someone had left a newspaper behind on the table . . . as usual, I looked first at the small ads. You can't imagine what it's like, plowing through the small ads, knowing . . . Oh well! . . ."

He waved a hand, as if to brush away a nightmare.

"And suddenly, there it was on page three. . . . My aunt's name . . . I couldn't take it in at first . . . it was just a few lines.

"Landlady strangled in bed in Bourg-la-Reine. Last night, Madame Juliette Boynet, a real-estate owner living in Bourg-la-Reine, was . . ."

"What time was this?"

"I don't know. It's a long time since I last owned a watch. . . . About half-past nine, maybe. I hurried back home. I told Hélène . . ."

"Your wife, you mean?"

"Yes . . . I told her that my aunt was dead, and I caught the bus."

"Did you by any chance stop for a drink first?"

"Just a small glass to buck me up. I couldn't understand why Cécile hadn't let me know."

"I presume you have expectations from your aunt?"

"Yes. My two sisters and I are her heirs. . . . I waited for a streetcar at the Châtelet and . . . But about Cécile . . . why was Cécile killed? The concierge has just told me."

"Cécile was killed because she knew the name of the murderer," Maigret said slowly.

The young man, showing no signs of calming down, stretched out his hand for the bottle of rum, but the Chief Superintendent intervened.

"No, that's enough. Sit down. What you could really do with is a cup of strong coffee."

"Are you insinuating . . .?"

His tone was aggressive. As far as he was concerned, Maigret was the enemy.

"You're not running away with the idea that I murdered my aunt and my sister, I hope?" he shouted, in a sudden spurt of rage.

Maigret made the mistake of not answering. It was not intentional. He was in the throes of one of his fits of abstraction. Or rather, to be more precise, he had just completed the imaginative leap needed to bring the interior of the apartment to life: the same apartment a few years earlier, the eccentric aunt, the three children, Cécile as an adolescent and her sister Berthe with her hair still loose, and Gérard planning to get away from it all by enlisting. . . .

He started. The young man had seized him by the collar of his coat, and was yelling:

"Why don't you answer? Do you believe . . . do you believe I . . . ?"

A powerful smell of spirits. Maigret shrank back, and seized the young man by the wrists.

"Easy, my boy," he murmured. "Relax . . ."

He had forgotten his own strength, and was holding the boy's wrists in a grip of steel.

"You're hurting me!" he whimpered.

At long last, his eyes overflowed with tears.

Part Two

One

Was there an epidemic of some sort in Bourg-la-Reine? Maigret could easily have found out but, the question having once crossed his mind, he gave no further thought to it. The undertaker's man would no doubt have told him that deaths occur in waves, that sometimes five days would go by with not a single hearse, either of the luxury or of the plainer variety, being taken out on the road, and that this lull might be followed by a period of hectic demand.

On this particular morning, the undertaker's resources were fully stretched, so much so that one of the two horses harnessed to Juliette Boynet's hearse was not trained for the job, and ten times at least attempted to break into a trot, thus imparting a somewhat jerky and hasty tempo to the procession, not at all in keeping with the funereal dignity of the occasion.

The arrangements for the funeral had been undertaken by a man named Monfils, an insurance agent from Luçon. No sooner had the press reported the murder of Juliette Boynet than he turned up in Paris, dressed in deep mourning (doubtless he had the outfit put by from some former occasion), and from then on this tall, thin, wan figure, sporting a red nose as a result of a cold caught on the train, was very much to the fore at all times.

He was Juliette Boynet's first cousin.

"I know what I'm talking about, Chief Superintendent. It was understood from way back that she would leave us something, and she agreed to stand godmother to our eldest child. . . . I'm sure there must be a will in existence. If none has been found, it may be that there are those who have an interest in causing it to disappear. . . .

What's more, I intend to register my claim with the court. . . ."

He had insisted on a grand funeral with all the trimmings, including the setting up of a memorial chapel in the apartment on the fifth floor, and the departure of the procession from the funeral parlor.

"We are not in the habit, in our family, of burying our dead on the cheap. . . ."

This very morning he had been to the station to collect his wife, also in deep mourning, and his five sons, all with unruly fair hair, who were now following the coffin, each carrying his hat, in descending order of size.

The traffic was at its heaviest on the main roads at this time of day, trucks mostly returning from the central market in endless file, nose to tail. It was a clear, sunny day, but there was a sharp nip in the air. People were stamping their feet and keeping their hands in their pockets.

Maigret had not had any sleep the previous night. He had sat up with Lucas, keeping watch on his gang of Poles in the room overlooking Rue de Birague. During the past three days, ever since Cécile's death, he had been gloomy and irritable. He was beginning to lose patience with the Poles, who were preventing him from giving his whole mind to the Bourg-la-Reine murders. By seven o'clock in the morning his mind was made up:

"You wait here! I'm going to pinch the first one to come out. . . ."

"Watch it, Chief. . . . They're armed. . . ."

He shrugged, went into the Hôtel des Arcades, mounted the stairs, and waited. A quarter of an hour later, the bedroom door opened. A giant of a man went to the stairs. Maigret flung himself upon him from behind, and the two men rolled over and over together until they reached the ground floor.

At last, having managed to fasten handcuffs on his

quarry, the Chief Superintendent got up. He blew his whistle, and Inspector Torrence came running.

"Take him to the Quai . . . I'll leave the job of grilling him to you. . . . Keep at it till he talks . . . understood? . . . Take it in relays, if necessary. I want a full confession."

He dusted himself down, and then went into a bar and had croissants and coffee laced with brandy at the counter.

Everyone in the Police Judiciaire knew that, at times like these, it was wiser not to cross him. Madame Maigret, for her part, dared not even ask him what time he would be home for his meals.

There he stood on the sidewalk, with his back to the window of the grocer's, looking sullen and smoking his pipe in little angry puffs. The press had written up the case, and there was a small crowd of spectators, not to mention half a dozen reporters and one or two photographers. The two hearses were drawn up in front of the house, first Juliette Boynet's and then Cécile's. Madame "Saving-Your-Presence," saying that it was the least they could do, had organized a collection among the tenants for a wreath.

TO OUR LANDLADY, WHO WILL BE SADLY MISSED

Beside the Monfilses, representing the family of Juliette Boynet, née Cazenove, there was another group representing the deceased husband, the Boynets and the Machepieds, who lived in Paris.

The two rival factions glowered at one another. Boynet and Machepied also claimed that they had been robbed, saying that the old woman had promised, after her husband's death, that part of her fortune would one day revert to his relations. They had turned up in force the previous night at police headquarters and, as they were persons of some standing, one of them being a city councilor, had been received by the Chief Commissioner himself.

"Tell me, Maigret . . . these gentlemen claim that

there is a will. I've told them again and again that the apartment has been thoroughly searched, but it makes no difference."

They had a grudge against Maigret, they had a grudge against Monfils, they had a grudge against Juliette. In other words, everyone felt cheated, Gérard Pardon most of all. He spoke not a word to anyone, and looked more distraught than ever.

Having no money, he had not been able to afford mourning clothes. Instead of an overcoat, he wore an old khaki mackintosh with a black armband.

His sister Berthe kept close to him, troubled at seeing him so agitated. She was a plump little thing, pretty and well groomed. She had not thought it necessary to buy a dark hat instead of the cherry-red confection she was wearing.

Monsieur Dandurand was also present, accompanied by four or five very self-assured gentlemen, all expensively dressed and wearing numerous flashing rings, who had turned up in a sumptuous limousine. The Siveschis, too, were there in force, except for the mother, who was still in bed. Madame Piéchaud, the grocer, had left Madame Benoit in charge of the shop for a few minutes while she went upstairs and sprinkled holy water on the coffins.

The undertaker, who was anyway on edge because he had another funeral at eleven, could not make head or tail of the various factions, and was quite unable to ascertain who was representing the family officially. And the presence of the photographers was an added cause for alarm.

"Wait a minute, gentlemen, I beg you. . . . Can't you at least wait until the procession has formed!"

The last thing he wanted was a photograph of a chaotic procession in the papers!

Fingers were pointed at Maigret, but he appeared not to notice. As the two coffins were being brought out, he touched Gérard Pardon on the shoulder. The young man gave a start.

"Could you spare me a minute?" he whispered, taking him aside.

"What do you want this time?"

"Your wife must have told you that I called on her yesterday while you were out."

"You don't mean you've been searching our hovel!"

He sniggered. It was a painful, grating sound.

"Did you find what you were looking for?"

And when the Chief Superintendent replied that he had, Pardon stared at him in horror.

"Believe it or not, when your wife just happened to have her back to me, I took the liberty of digging my fingers into a flowerpot. . . . I'm a bit of a gardener in my spare time, you see, and there was something about those flowers that didn't look right to me! And look what I found buried in the recently disturbed soil."

He held out his hand, in the palm of which lay a small key, the key to the front door of Juliette Boynet's apartment.

"Odd, don't you think?" he went on. "And here's a coincidence . . . when I returned to my office a little while later, I found there was a locksmith waiting to see me, a locksmith who lives not a hundred yards from here, and who wished to inform me that he had cut a key similar to this one less than a fortnight ago."

"What does that prove?"

Gérard was trembling. He looked about him wildly, as though in search of help, and his glance rested on his sister's coffin being hoisted into the hearse by the men in black.

"Are you going to arrest me?"

"I don't know yet. . . ."

"If you questioned the locksmith, he must have told you that I got that key . . ."

He had got it from Cécile! The locksmith's statement had established that beyond doubt.

"On Monday, September twenty-fifth," he had stated, "a young woman of about thirty came into my workshop, produced a Yale key, and asked me if I could make her a copy. I said I would need the original key to work from. She objected that it was her only key, and that she would be needing it, so I made a wax impression. Next day, she came to collect the new key, and paid me twelve francs seventy-five centimes. . . . It was only when I read in the papers that Cécile Pardon had been murdered, and in particular when I learned from her description that she had a slight squint, that . . ."

The procession was beginning to move. The master of ceremonies bustled up to Gérard, waving his arms. Maigret whispered:

"We'll talk later. . . ."

Gérard and his sister Berthe were placed immediately behind the hearses, but they had not gone ten yards before Monfils, disputing their right of precedence, came forward to join them.

The Boynets and the Machepieds, less officious, scorned any hypocritical show of grief and followed behind, deep in discussion regarding the succession. Monsieur Dandurand and the gentlemen of the flashy rings came next, all except one, who brought up the rear of the procession, driving the big car.

From the start, on account of the temperamental horse, the pace was distinctly brisk. When the time came, however, to turn left off the main road for the church, there was a fearful snarl-up. All traffic was brought to a halt for several minutes, including three streetcars in a row.

In view of her condition, Gérard's wife was not present.

Her confinement was due within a week or less. Maigret had spent an hour with her the previous night, in their lodgings, comprising two rooms over a butcher's shop on Rue du Pas-de-la-Mule.

She was barely twenty-three years of age, yet her face was not youthful, but aged with the resignation of the poor. It was plain to see that she had tried, with all the inadequate means at her command, to make the two rooms habitable. Some of her possessions had no doubt already found their way to the pawnshop. Maigret noticed that the gas had been cut off.

"Gérard has always been unlucky," she sighed without rancor. "And yet he has many virtues. . . . He's a great deal more intelligent than many others who have good jobs. . . . Maybe that's his trouble?"

Her name was Hélène. Her father was working for a credit company. She had been too scared to let him know how things really stood in her house, and had led him to believe that Gérard was working, and that the marriage was a happy one.

"He may seem somewhat aggressive to you, but look at it from his point of view. Lately, everything has gone against him. He's out from morning till night, answering advertisements for jobs. . . . Surely you don't regard him as a suspect? He's the soul of honesty. Maybe it's just because he is so scrupulously honest that he's a failure. . . . Let me give you an example! In his last job, he worked in a shop selling vacuum cleaners. There was a break-in. Gérard suspected that one of his fellow employees was involved. He said nothing, but later the boss subjected him to a barrage of questions, making Gérard feel that he himself was under suspicion. And rather than involve anyone else, Gérard gave notice. . . .

"Oh, by all means make a thorough search! You won't find anything of interest here except bills . . ."

And the flowerpot on the window sill! Maigret had

noticed that the soil had been recently disturbed, although the geranium planted in it had long since died. While Hélène's attention was momentarily distracted, he had pounced. . . .

With his hands in his pockets, he strolled along the sidewalk on the edge of the procession, and so felt free to smoke his pipe.

At the tail end of the procession he observed the two Siveschi girls, Nouchi and Potsi, who were treating it as a festive occasion and relishing every detail. Madame "Saving-Your-Presence" had left her lodge in the charge of a neighbor for an hour or so, unaware that Maigret had posted an inspector on guard outside the building. She would be attending the service in the church, but not the burial. She was sensitive to drafts, on account of her stiff neck.

Suddenly the column came to an unscheduled halt. They all craned their necks and stood on tiptoe to find out what was happening.

Juliette Boynet and Cécile were victims of an unfortunate mischance. As their procession, which was running early, reached a crossroads, another funeral procession, this one running late, emerged from a side road and made for the church. There was no alternative but to wait. The horses stamped their feet. Several of the men left the column to go in search of a drink, and were seen a few minutes later coming out of a little café nearby, wiping their mouths.

Organ music could be heard, and behind, cars rumbling past on the Route Nationale 20. The priest galloped through the service at top speed, and it was not long before the church doors were flung wide open.

Et ne nos inducas in tentationem . . .

The master of ceremonies, in a cocked hat, ran back and forth alongside his flock like a sheepdog.

Sed libera nos a malo . . .

Amen. . . .

Before the first lot had all come out, Juliette Boynet's mourners began entering the church. There was room for only one of the two coffins on the bier. Cécile's was set down at the back, on the tiled floor.

"Libera nos, Domine," chanted the priest.

There was a creaking of shoes, a scraping of chairs, a cool breeze blew in through the wide open door at the back, beyond which could be seen the sunlit street. Gérard, in the front row, looked restlessly about him. Was it Maigret he was searching for? Charles Dandurand's companions, conducting themselves very correctly, dropped hundred-franc notes into the poorbox. Berthe, conspicuous in her cherry-red hat, watched her brother anxiously, as if she feared he might do something foolish.

Pater noster . . .

The magnesium flare of an agency photographer suddenly flashed, causing everyone to start.

Maigret, huddled in his heavy overcoat with the velvet collar, was leaning against a stone pillar, his lips moving as if in prayer. And, indeed, he might well have been praying for poor Cécile, who had sat waiting for him so long in the "aquarium" at the Quai des Orfèvres.

For the past three days, his colleagues had scarcely dared address a word to him. Heavy and lowering, he went to and fro in the building, chewing the stem of his pipe and brooding furiously.

"No progress?" the Chief had inquired the previous night.

His only reply had been a look so miserable and baffled that it spoke louder than words.

"It's no good fretting, my dear fellow. . . . You're bound to get a lead soon."

The Apostles in the stained-glass windows glowed in the sunlight. Maigret's glance, for no apparent reason, kept returning to the figure of Saint Luke, whom the artist had portrayed with a square, brown beard.

Et ne nos inducas in tentationem . . .

The priest was rushing through the service at such speed as to suggest that there was another funeral procession champing at the door. The horse that had not been properly trained in funeral procedures kept whinnying every few minutes, and the sound, re-echoing under the stone vaults, seemed like a joyful affirmation of life. . . .

What could have induced Cécile to have an extra key to the apartment cut without her aunt's knowledge a fortnight ago? Was it she who had given it to her brother? If so . . .

He could see her still, motionless in the waiting room with her handbag on her lap, prepared to sit there for hours, not moving a muscle.

Maigret recalled his own thoughts:

"Either she was called away by someone she knew and trusted, or she was led to believe that she was being taken to see me."

Her brother?

Gérard had never taken his eyes off him during the whole of the service. Every now and then Berthe would pat his arm to reassure him. Embarrassed, the Chief Superintendent avoided the young man's gaze.

"This way, gentlemen. . . . Hurry along, please!"

At the cemetery, too, there was a great deal of bustle that day. They hastened past the family mausoleums and individual stone monuments, and before long had reached the new section with its slabs of clay surmounted by wooden crosses. The two coffins were hoisted onto trolleys and wheeled along the narrow pathways, followed by the mourners walking in single file.

"Might I have a word with you, Chief Superintendent? When would be convenient?"

"Where are you staying?"

"At the Hôtel du Centre, on Boulevard Montparnasse. . . ."

It was Monfils, who had caught up with Maigret as they made their way to the graveside.

"I'll probably look in on you sometime today."

"Wouldn't you rather I came to your office?"

"I don't know what my schedule will be."

And Maigret hurried forward to catch up with Berthe, who had been temporarily separated from her brother in the crowd.

"You shouldn't let him out of your sight. He's terribly overwrought. Try to persuade him to go back with you to your place. I'll come and see him there. . . ."

She assented with a flicker of her eyelashes. She was a pretty girl, a plump little creature, seeming infinitely remote from the dramatic events of the past few days.

"Excuse me, Chief Superintendent . . ."

Maigret turned to face one of Monsieur Dandurand's friends.

"Could you spare me a minute or two? There's a quiet little bistro just across the road from the cemetery. . . ."

Leading the procession was a deacon, attended by a small choirboy, who galloped along as fast as his short legs could carry him, in spite of his inconveniently long black skirts and heavy hobnailed boots. Bending over the open grave, the deacon turned the pages of his prayer book, then, his lips still moving, flung the first spadeful of earth on the coffins. Gérard and his cousin Monfils held out their hands simultaneously. There were too many heads in the way for Maigret to see which of them managed to get in first.

Suddenly, the gathering broke up in disorder. Nouchi bustled across to the Chief Superintendent and subjected him to a shameless stare. He would not have been surprised if she had asked him for his autograph, as she would a film star.

The bistro stood in the middle of a monument mason's yard. When Maigret pushed open the door, he found Dandurand's smart friends already seated at a table. They all stood up.

"Forgive me for taking up your time like this. . . . What will you have? Waiter! The same for the Chief Superintendent."

Charles Dandurand was there with them, smooth and gray, as gray as the tombstones.

"Take a seat, Chief Superintendent. We would gladly have gone to your office, but maybe it's better . . ."

All the big bosses who were in the habit of forgathering every evening at Albert's place were there, every bit as self-possessed as a board of directors seated around a table covered in green baize.

"Cheers! Let's not beat about the bush. Chief Superintendent Cassieux can vouch for us. He knows we are on the level. . . ."

The big limousine was waiting at the gates, and a group of kids were clustered around it, admiring the chromium fittings that glinted in the sunlight.

"It's about poor Juliette, needless to say. As you know, the law, in its moral wisdom, does not recognize the legality of any transactions entered into in connection with our sort of enterprise. We have to manage as best we can among ourselves. The fact is that Juliette had a share in at least a dozen establishments, not counting those in Béziers and on Rue d'Antin, which she wholly owned. Monsieur Charles will tell you that we have met here to consider our position and future plans."

The others nodded gravely. Monsieur Charles sat motionless, with his smooth, bloodless hands palms down on the table.

"The same again, waiter! . . . Do you appreciate what these enterprises represent, Chief Superintendent, in terms of hard cash? Something over three thousand big ones, in other words, more than three million francs. Now, the last thing we want is trouble. Apparently she didn't leave a will. Quite rightly, Monsieur Charles doesn't want any fuss. So we wondered if you could advise us as to how we should proceed. . . . Monsieur Charles has already been approached by two fellows. First of all, there's that death's head, Monfils, who is here with his brood, and then there's the young lady's brother, the boy Gérard. They're after the money, the pair of them. Not that we are raising any objection, but at the same time we've got to know who legally gets the dough. Well, that's how matters stand at present. You must realize that one can't close down highly profitable establishments, just because . . ."

Abruptly, the speaker rose to his feet, and took Maigret by the arm.

"A private word with you, if you permit . . ."

He led Maigret into a room at the back.

"I am what I am, and I don't pretend to be anything else. . . . All the same, there's one point on which you can safely take my word and that of my colleagues, and that is that Monsieur Charles has always played straight. The old lady's papers have disappeared, but we're not the sort to niggle over a signature. I said three million . . . I could be underestimating. But, documents or no documents, no one is going to touch a penny until you give the word. . . ."

"I'll have to consult with my superiors," replied Maigret.

"One moment . . . there is something else, but it concerns my colleagues as much as myself."

They returned to the larger front room.

"Well, Chief Superintendent, here it is. . . . We have decided to put twenty grand at your disposal, to help in the search for the bastard who did old Juliette in. Is that all right? Is it enough? Are we agreed? . . . Monsieur Charles will hand over the dough."

The former lawyer, under the misapprehension that the time had come, drew from his pocket a wallet stuffed to bursting point.

"Not now," said the Chief Superintendent, cutting him short. "I shall have to refer the matter. . . . Waiter! My bill. Oh, yes! I'm sorry, but I must insist. . . ."

And, as he paid for his drinks, the man who had appointed himself spokesman for the others grumbled:

"As you prefer . . . if you don't like our club . . . !"

Maigret went out of the bistro with a glow in his chest from having drunk two apéritifs. He had not gone ten paces when he came to an abrupt halt.

He found himself face to face with Gérard and his sister Berthe. Gérard was looking more distraught than ever. Berthe gave the Chief Superintendent a look which plainly said:

I did all I could to get him away. . . . See for yourself. . . . I can't do a thing with him. . . .

As for Cécile's brother, he had contrived to knock back a few drinks, and he reeked of spirits. With trembling lips and in a voice uncontrollably shrill, he shouted defiantly:

"And now, Chief Superintendent, I'd be obliged if you would kindly explain yourself . . ."

The gravediggers were overworked. They were needed elsewhere, and Cécile's coffin lay uncovered, except for a few spadefuls of yellow earth.

Two

"Go right in, my girl."

It was certainly not in character, but Maigret, without realizing it, felt an urge to lay his hand on Berthe Pardon's plump shoulder. This sort of quasi-paternal response is common enough in elderly men, and seldom arouses comment. But the Chief Superintendent had no doubt been clumsy, because the girl turned around and stared at him in amazement, as if to say:

You, too . . . !

He felt a little foolish.

Her brother had preceded them into the apartment, which had been stripped only a few minutes before of its funereal draperies. They had encountered the deputy undertaker's men with their gear in the hall on their way up.

Maigret was just about to follow the others inside when a voice with a slight foreign accent murmured in his ear:

"Could I have a word with you, Chief Superintendent?"

He recognized Nouchi, dressed for the funeral in a black suit several sizes too small and too tight for her. No doubt it had been made two or three years before her figure had reached maturity, and it accentuated her precocity.

"Later," he said irritably. He had no patience with this impudent chit.

"It's very urgent, really it is!"

Maigret went into the late Juliette Boynet's apartment and said grumpily, as he shut the door:

"Urgent or not, it will have to wait."

Having got Gérard where he wanted him, he intended to straighten things out with him once and for all. That

Berthe was there as well was all to the good, he felt. The old woman's apartment was a more suitable setting for this particular confrontation than his office at the Quai des Orfèvres. The atmosphere of the place was already having its effect on Gérard's nerves. He was gazing with a kind of anguish at the walls, so recently stripped of their black draperies, and breathing in the smell of candles and flowers, like the stale smell of death itself.

As for Berthe Pardon, she was as much at home here as behind her counter at the Galéries Lafayette or in the little fixed-price restaurant where she usually had her meals.

Her round face, still childlike, exuded serenity and that inner contentment which some believe to be the expression of an easy conscience. She seemed the very quintessence of girlhood, untouched not by sin only but by the very notion of sin.

"Sit down, my dears," said Maigret, taking his pipe out of his pocket.

Gérard was far too tense to settle in one of the sitting-room armchairs. In marked contrast to his sister, he was on edge the whole time, his mind in a turmoil, his eyes never still.

"Why don't you say straight out that you suspect me of having murdered my aunt and sister?" he asked, his lips trembling. "Just because I'm poor, and because I've always been dogged by ill-luck . . . What do you care about upsetting my wife, who is expecting a child any moment now and who, anyway, has never been strong? . . . You take advantage of my absence to go ferreting about in our lodgings. You made quite sure first that I would be out, didn't you?"

"That's right," said Maigret, gazing at the pictures on the walls as he lit his pipe.

"Because you had no search warrant . . . because you knew I would never have permitted it."

"No! Of course not!"

Berthe took off the fur piece she was wearing around her neck. It was a strip of pine marten, too long and too narrow. The Chief Superintendent was impressed by the whiteness and smoothness of her throat.

"Have you so much as asked that phony Monfils where he was on the night of the murder? I'm quite sure you haven't, because he is . . ."

"I intend to put that very question to him this afternoon. . . ."

"In that case, you can also ask him if it isn't true that my sisters and I have been cheated of our rights from start to finish."

He pointed to a somewhat faded enlargement of a photograph of a woman.

"That's my mother," he declaimed. "Cécile was very like her. . . . Not only in looks, but in character. You wouldn't understand their sort of humility, their dread of stepping out of line, of taking more than their due . . . their unwholesome craving for self-sacrifice. That was what my poor sister was like, and she was a slave all her life. That's true, Berthe, isn't it?"

"Quite true," agreed the girl. "Aunt Juliette treated her like a servant."

"What the Chief Superintendent doesn't realize . . ."

Maigret had difficulty in suppressing a smile, for there was one thing that this seething young man could not see, and that was that he himself suffered from an inferiority complex. But this sense of inferiority irked him so much that, in order to shake it off, he went to the other extreme and adopted an aggressive and defiant posture.

"My mother was the older sister. She was forty-eight when my aunt met Boynet, who was a wealthy man. After their parents died, the two daughters lived together in Fontenay, on the income they inherited jointly. Now, what happened was this. In order to marry Boynet, my aunt had to have a dowry, so she got my mother to agree to give up her share of the inheritance. Everyone in the family knows that, and, unless he is a liar, Monfils will confirm it. So you see, it was thanks to my mother that Aunt Juliette was able to make such a good match.

" *'I'll make it up to you one day . . . you can rest assured that I'll never forget. . . . After I'm married . . .'*

"Not a penny! After she was married, she looked down on her sister as being too poor to be introduced to her grand new friends, so my poor mother had to go to work in a shop in Fontenay. She married one of the supervisors in the store. He was already in poor health. And she had to go on working . . .

"Then we were born, and the most that my aunt could be persuaded to do was to stand godmother to Cécile. And do you know what she sent her for her First Communion? A hundred francs. And she with a husband who already owned at least ten apartment buildings.

" *'You have nothing to fear, Emilie,'* she wrote to my mother. *'If anything should happen to you, I will take care of the children.'*

"First, my father died and, not long after, my mother. By then, Aunt Juliette was a widow, and she had recently moved to this apartment, though she occupied the whole floor in those days.

"It was our cousin Monfils who brought us from Fontenay. . . . You wouldn't remember, Berthe . . . you were too young.

" *'Good God! How skinny they are!'* exclaimed Aunt Juliette when she saw us. *'You'd think my poor sister had starved them. . . .'*

"She was critical of everything about us, our outer clothes and underwear, our worn shoes, our manners . . .

"As for Cécile, who was nearly grown up, she treated her like a servant from the start. She wanted to send me to trade school, saying that the poor should earn a living with their hands. If I came home with a tear in my trousers, I would never hear the end of it. I was an ungrateful brat, I didn't appreciate all that she was doing for me and my sisters. . . . Mark her words, I would come to a wretched end . . .

"Cécile suffered in silence. The maid was fired. Why should she keep a servant, with my sister there to do all the work? . . . Would you like to see the sort of clothes she made us wear?"

He went across to a cabinet and got a photograph of all three of them. Cécile was in black, as Maigret had known her, her hair unbecomingly drawn back into a tight knot; Berthe, plump as a puppy, in a dress too long for a child of her age; and Gérard, aged fourteen or fifteen, wearing a suit that had certainly not been made to measure.

"I decided to enlist in the army, and she never sent me so much as a five-franc piece to tide me over till the end of the month. . . . My buddies used to get parcels from home, cigarettes and things. All my life, I've had to look on at what other people had."

"How old were you when you ceased to live with your aunt?" Maigret asked, turning to the girl.

"Sixteen," she replied. "I applied all on my own for a job in a department store. They asked me my age, and I said I was eighteen."

"When I got married," Gérard went on, "my aunt sent me a silver cake slicer . . . Later, when I was desperate for money, I sold it, and all I could get for it was thirty francs. Cécile barely got enough to eat, and yet our aunt was a rich woman. And now that she's dead, I'm the one who's being made to suffer. You're the same as all the rest."

It was painful to look at him, he was so eaten up with bitterness and resentment.

"Were you never tempted to kill your aunt?" asked Maigret, so matter-of-factly that it gave the girl a start.

"If I said 'yes,' that would be as good as telling you I strangled her, wouldn't it? Well, yes, I often wished her dead. Unfortunately, I'm too much of a coward. . . . Well, there it is, you can think what you like. Arrest me, if that's what you want, it will only be the last of many injustices."

Berthe glanced at the little wrist watch she was wearing.

"Can I be of any further use to you, Chief Superintendent?"

"Why do you ask?"

"It is lunchtime. My friend will be waiting for me outside the store."

This reference to her lover did not detract from her air of virginal innocence.

"You have my address: Twenty-two Rue Ordener. I'm nearly always at home in the evenings after seven, except when we go out to see a movie. . . . What are you going to do with Gérard? He always carries on like this. You mustn't take him too seriously. Are you all right for money, Gérard? Give Hélène a kiss from me. Tell her I'll drop by and see her tomorrow or the day after. They've given me three days off at the store."

On her way to the door, she turned and smiled at the two men before going out.

"And this is what we've come down to," concluded Gérard. "Her boy friend is a married man! If my poor mother . . ."

"Tell me, why did Cécile give you this key?"

"You really want to know? I'll tell you, but you're not going to like it. She gave it to me because the police weren't doing their job! Because, when a poor person goes to them for help, they won't even listen! Cécile went to see you several times, even you wouldn't dare deny that. She told you that she was frightened, that there was something going on in this apartment that she didn't understand. And what did you do? You made fun of her. You sent along an absurd little sergeant a couple of times, who did nothing but pace up and down outside the house. When Cécile, by then convinced beyond any doubt that someone was getting into the sitting room at night, called on you again, she could sense that the whole department was having a good laugh at her expense. So much so that the inspectors took it in relays to go and peer at her in the waiting room."

Maigret listened with bowed head.

"It was then that she had a key cut. She asked me . . ."

"Sorry to interrupt! Where did you and your sister use to meet?"

"In the street! When I needed to see her . . ."

"To ask her for money?"

"Yes! To ask her for money, that's right. I daresay you're very pleased with yourself for having found that out! She did, in fact, occasionally slip me a few francs. It was never very much, just what she was able to scrape together, as they say, out of the housekeeping. I used to wait for her at the corner, when I knew she would be going out to do her shopping! . . . Does that satisfy you? I'm only too happy to oblige! . . . She gave me the key about ten days ago. She asked me to check on the apartment from time to time at night, to try and find out what was going on. . . ."

"And did you?"

"No . . . I couldn't, on account of my wife. The doctor feared a premature confinement. I intended to look into it later."

"How would you have got into the building?"

"Cécile had thought of everything. Every evening at seven o'clock, the concierge goes upstairs with the mail. She always stops for a few minutes to chat with the Deséglises. They're the third-floor tenants in the apartment on the left. All I had to do was to slip in then. . . ."

"What about your aunt?"

"Oh, what the hell! I know every word I say will be used

against me. It's all too easy. Well, then, here goes. My aunt suffered from pains in the legs, and, every evening at about that time, she had hot air massage, which apparently relieved the pain. My sister used an electric dryer, like those one sees at the hairdresser's. They make quite a lot of noise. . . . All I had to do was let myself in with my key and go and hide under Cécile's bed. Are you satisfied? And now, if you don't mind, I'm hungry and my wife is expecting me home. You've scared her enough already, going to see her like that. If I'm not back soon, she'll think . . . So, unless you intend to arrest me here and now, I'll thank you to let me go. As for her money, which is ours by right, we'll see whether . . ."

He turned his head away, but not soon enough to prevent Maigret from seeing the tears of rage that were running down his cheeks.

"You are at liberty to go," said the Chief Superintendent.

"Is that so?" exclaimed the young man, with heavy irony. "So I'm not to be arrested just yet? You are too kind. How can I ever thank you. . . ."

Gérard was not sure that he had caught the words aright, but as he made for the door he thought he heard Maigret say:

"Silly ass!"

Was Nouchi still hoping to succeed in seducing the Chief Superintendent? She was doing her best, at any rate, with a curious blend of cunning and artlessness. She even, as she sat down opposite him, went so far as to hitch her skirt well up above her bony knees.

"Where were you?" he asked, as grumpily as he knew how.

"In the street."

"What were you doing there?"

"Talking to a friend. . . ."

"Are you sure this was on the night of the murder?"

"It's in my diary. . . . Every night, I record the events of the day in my diary."

Maigret reflected that he himself no doubt also featured in this crazy girl's diary. Nouchi was one of those girls who fall in love with every man they see, the policeman on the beat, the neighbor whom they encounter every day at the same hour, the film star whom they have never met in the flesh, the notorious murderer, of whom they have only read. For the time being, Maigret was the star!

"I can't tell you the name of my friend, because he's a married man. . . ."

Indeed? Well, Berthe, serene little Berthe, with her cherry-red hat, was also having an affair with a married man!

"So you were out in the street, not far from this building. . . . Weren't you afraid your parents might see you?"

"It wouldn't bother my parents. . . . They're quite decent. . . ."

"And you claim you saw Gérard Pardon entering the building?"

"He was dressed exactly as he was today, in the same raincoat and the same gray hat with the turned-down brim. . . . He looked around, and then bolted inside."

"What time was this?"

"Seven o'clock in the evening. I'm quite sure of that, because the postman had just made his last delivery."

"Thank you very much."

"It's important, don't you think?"

"I don't know."

"But surely, if Cécile's brother was in the building that night . . ."

"Thank you, mademoiselle."

"Isn't there anything else you want to ask me?"

"No."

She stood up. Still hopeful, she added:

"You can rely on me to help you all I can. I know all that goes on in this house. . . . I could tell you . . ."

"Thanks."

As he went to the door she brushed against him; he could feel the tension in her body.

"Won't I have to go to police headquarters, to have my statement taken down in writing?"

"Not until you receive an official summons."

"*Au revoir*, Chief Superintendent."

"Good-by."

And Maigret, having locked the door and put the key in his pocket, went down the stairs. Inspector Jourdan was still on guard outside the building. Maigret signaled to him to carry on, and went off in search of a taxi.

During the whole of lunch in his apartment on Boulevard Richard-Lenoir, his wife could not get a word out of him. He sat with his elbows on the table, scattering breadcrumbs on the cloth and champing his food noisily. These were all ominous signs.

"You can't blame yourself if this girl Cécile . . ." she ventured, addressing him by the formal *vous*, as she was apt to do at such times. Had anyone else been present just then, she would have referred to her husband as "the Chief Superintendent," or even, though this was more unusual, as "Monsieur Maigret."

Had he even noticed that he had just eaten a luscious *crême caramel*? No sooner had he wiped his mouth with his napkin than he was taking his overcoat, stiff as a soldier's cape, from the stand. She could tell from his manner that there was nothing to be gained by asking him when he would be back.

"Hôtel du Centre, Boulevard Montparnasse," he snapped at the taxi driver.

It was a quiet little hotel, mainly patronized by regulars

from the provinces, who tended always to come to Paris on a particular day of the week. It smelled of veal in a savory sauce and fresh-baked cookies.

"Monsieur Monfils is expecting me."

"He's waiting for you in the conservatory."

There really was a conservatory, or at least a glassed-in enclosure with a lot of greenery, a rockery, and a fountain.

Monsieur Monfils, still dressed in deep mourning, his nose red and running, was sitting in a wicker armchair with a handkerchief in his hand, smoking a cigar. With him was another man, whose face seemed familiar to Maigret.

"Allow me to introduce my legal adviser, Maître Leloup. . . . It is Maître Leloup who will in future be looking after my interests in Paris."

The lawyer was as fat as Monfils was thin, and there was an ample glass of brandy on a table within reach of his hand.

"How do you do, Chief Superintendent. Please be seated. My client . . ."

"One moment!" interposed Maigret. "I was not aware that Monsieur Monfils was in need of a lawyer at this stage."

"I am here merely to represent his financial interests, I assure you. The present situation appears to be somewhat confused, and until the will has been found . . ."

"How do you know that any will exists?"

"Oh, come now, it stands to reason! A woman as rich and hardheaded as Madame Boynet, formerly Cazenove, would surely not fail to . . ."

At this juncture, Madame Monfils and her five sons irrupted into the conservatory, the boys following one another in descending order of height.

"Please excuse us," murmured the lady, with a suitably doleful smile. "We're leaving, Henri! We've barely time to get to the station. . . . *Au revoir*, Chief Superintendent. *Au revoir*, Maître Leloup. You won't be staying on much longer in Paris, will you, Henri?"

The children embraced their father, one by one. The porter waited with the luggage. At long last they left, and Henri Monfils, having poured two glasses of brandy and handed one to Maigret without a word, began:

"I thought it my duty, Chief Superintendent, my duty to my family in particular, to consult a lawyer, so that he could represent me in any future dealings with you, and . . ."

Monfils's nose was running. He got his handkerchief out of his pocket only just in time. As he was doing so, the Chief Superintendent got up and grabbed his bowler hat, which he had put down on a chair. Monfils stared at him in amazement. "But . . . Where are you going?"

"If Maître Leloup has any statement to make, he is welcome to come and do so in my office," retorted Maigret. "Good day, gentlemen."

Henri Monfils was dumfounded.

"What's the matter? . . . What's got into him?"

And his legal adviser, leaning back in his wicker armchair and warming his brandy snifter in the palm of his plump hand, murmured reassuringly:

"Don't take any notice. . . . It's just his way. . . . These police johnnies don't like conducting their business through a professional intermediary. He was annoyed at finding me here. Leave it to me, and I'll . . ."

He interrupted himself to give all his attention to biting off the end of the cigar which his client had presented to him.

"Take my word for it . . ."

The early editions of the evening papers, which had just come off the presses, ran pictures of the funeral. One of them featured Maigret in a prominent position on the edge of Cécile's grave, next to the priest, who was sprinkling holy water.

If they could have seen Maigret, with his hands in his pockets and his pipe clenched between his teeth, lumbering down Boulevard Montparnasse with a thoroughly disgruntled air, stopping outside a movie house plastered in brightly colored posters, and, after some little hesitation, going up to the box office and handing over some money, they would have been very much astonished. They being Jourdan, pounding the beat outside the house in Bourg-la-Reine, where lights were beginning to show in the windows; the head of the Sûreté, speaking on the telephone in his office, and wondering what on earth to say in reply to the Public Prosecutor's questions; and Madame Maigret, busy polishing her brass.

Having bought his ticket, Maigret obediently followed the usherette, in her black silk dress with the Peter Pan collar, as she led him, shining her flashlight, up the narrow stairs.

"Excuse me. . . . Excuse me. . . . Excuse me. . . ."

He squeezed past the row of occupied seats, uncomfortably aware that he was creating a disturbance and treading on a great many toes.

He had no idea what film he was seeing. Booming voices, seemingly coming from nowhere, filled the auditorium, and on the screen a ship's captain tossed a girl onto his bunk.

"So you came here to spy on me . . ."

"Have pity on me, Captain Brown. If not for my sake, at least for . . ."

"Excuse me," whispered a shy little voice to the right of the Chief Superintendent.

And Maigret could feel the woman next to him pulling something from under him. He had sat down on part of her coat.

Three

Maigret was feeling warm, "warm and cozy," as he used to say when he was a child, and if the lights had suddenly been turned on, he would have appeared, leaning back, huddled in his overcoat, with his hands in his pockets and his eyes half closed, as the very incarnation of contentment.

But in fact it was just a device, a little game that he played with himself whenever he became so saturated with a single problem that he felt incapable of further reasoning. If it had been summer, he would have been sitting in the sun on a café terrace with a glass of beer in front of him, his eyes half shut, simmering.

When they had put in central heating at the Quai des Orfèvres, and the Chief Superintendent had sought and obtained permission to keep his old anthracite stove, some of the young inspectors had raised their eyebrows. Had they but known, it was just the old familiar game. Whenever things were going badly, whenever he had teased and worried a particular problem until it had lost all meaning and become a tangle of loose ends, Maigret would fill his stove to bursting point and then after poking it and turning it full on, toast himself on both sides in front of it. Little by little he would be filled with a glow of well-being, his eyelids would begin to prickle, and he would see everything around him through a haze, which was not entirely due to the smoke of his never extinguished pipe.

In this torpid bodily state, his mind was freed, as in dreams, to wander at will, sometimes in pursuit of will-o'-

the-wisps, but occasionally along paths which reason alone could never have discovered.

Madame Maigret had never caught on. Often, after an evening at the movies, she would touch him on the arm and say with a sigh:

"You slept through it again, Maigret. . . . I can't see the point of spending twelve francs for a seat when you have a perfectly good bed at home."

The auditorium was pitch-dark, heated by the warmth generated by hundreds of human bodies, pulsating with the lives of all these people, so close together and yet unknown to one another. Above their heads ran the long, triangular beam of pallid light from the projection room, a focus for tobacco smoke.

If anyone had asked him what the film was about . . . As if that mattered. . . . He watched the images flickering on the screen without attempting to relate to them in any way. Then, conscious of a slight rustle nearby, he looked down.

This powerful man, who for nearly thirty years had, in a sense, been involved with the uttermost frenzy of human passion, with murder, that is, was a puritan. In the semidarkness, he could sense the movements of the woman next to him and her companion's on the other side, though all he could see was the man's pale hand. He gave a brief shocked cough. Earlier, when she had pulled her coat from under him, he had had the impression that she was very young. She was motionless. Her face was white, like the man's hand, like the patch of thigh that he was uncovering, while keeping his eyes firmly fixed on the screen.

Uncomfortably, the Chief Superintendent coughed again, twice.

The lovers ignored him. The girl could not have been much older than Nouchi.

Come to think of it, when Nouchi had seen Gérard

going into the building in Bourg-la-Reine, at seven o'clock at night . . . But had she really seen him? She, too, had been with a man in the dark, pressed up against a wall, no doubt . . .

The soft sound of a kiss beside him. . . . He could almost taste the moist, unfamiliar mouth. . . . He slumped deeper inside the collar of his overcoat.

Not long ago, Nouchi had been impudently provocative. . . . If he had been so inclined . . . Was it a common feature of adolescent girlhood, this inclination to throw themselves at the head of any older man, just because he was fairly well known or generally respected?

I bet he's a lot older than she is! he mused, with reference to his neighbor's companion.

He was not thinking, but leaving his mind open to any stray scrap of an idea that might come into it, without any attempt at order or coherence.

Had the little Hungarian girl been lying about Monsieur Charles? Surely not. Dandurand was just the sort of man to spy on a young girl through a crack in the door and to show her pornographic photographs. As for Nouchi, she would be all too ready to lead him on to the limit, knowing that, in the last resort, she could shout for help. . . .

The thing that really worried him was her claim that she had seen Gérard Pardon going into the building at seven in the evening, at the very time when Madame "Saving-Your-Presence" was chatting with the Deséglises, out of sight of the stairs.

After she has made her statement officially . . .

So the word of a perverse kid would be enough to send a man to prison, and who could tell . . . ?

He was troubled, ill at ease. It was not only the thought of Gérard slinking out of the door leading onto Boulevard Arago in the small hours. . . . He was still watching the screen. . . . He frowned. For the last few minutes, he had been conscious of something unnatural. Suddenly he realized what it was: the lips of the characters in the film were moving, but the spoken words did not correspond. In fact, the lips were forming English words, while the sound track was in French. In other words, the film was dubbed.

The couple next to him were behaving more and more outrageously, but the Chief Superintendent's mind was elsewhere. What was it that had been baffling him for the past three days? That was the key question, though he had not realized it. Now he understood. There was a jarring note somewhere in this case. Somewhere, something did not ring true. What was it? As yet, he had no idea.

With eyes half shut, he could see the wedge-shaped building on the Route Nationale more clearly than if he had been standing outside it, looking in at the windows of the bicycle shop and the widow Piéchaud's grocery store. In fact, as he had discovered the previous day, she was not a widow. Her husband had left her for a woman of easy virtue, as the phrase is, and she considered this so shameful that she chose to be known as a widow.

But Madame "Saving-Your-Presence," in her cozy lodge, with her head askew and her neck enveloped in surgical wadding . . .

Just because she herself had never opened the front door to a stranger, it had been too hastily assumed that no one had entered or left the building that night.

Now, it had been proved that it was possible to get into the building at seven o'clock in the evening without being seen by the concierge. Who was to say that there were not other times in the day when the same conditions obtained?

Up there on the top floor, that eccentric old woman, Juliette Boynet, had chosen to make a mystery of the visits of Charles Dandurand when he called to discuss her investments in enterprises which were, to say the least, morally dubious. It was all very unsavory but, human nature being what it is, not so very surprising. She was not the first of her kind that Maigret had encountered in the course of his career.

He had met others like Dandurand as well.

What was it, then, that did not ring true, that was contrary to his experience of human nature?

The old woman had been strangled, soon after Dandurand's departure, as she was about to get into bed. She had still been wearing one stocking.

Was one to suppose that there was a third key in existence, and that it was in the possession of Monsieur Charles? Was one to believe that he had gone into the apartment with the intention of killing the old woman?

He, too, was rich. Juliette was worth more to him alive than dead.

One of his underworld cronies? They were not beginners, faceless hooligans game for anything, but successful men, substantial property owners who would not wish to be mixed up in anything downright criminal.

They were telling the truth when they claimed that this business was a nuisance and an embarrassment to them.

Gérard Pardon . . . ?

By this time, the two next to Maigret were frankly going too far, just as if they had the whole of the dark auditorium to themselves.

Maigret had to keep firm control on himself or he would have shouted:

"Stop it, damn you!"

. . . Gérard, creeping into his sister's bedroom at seven in the evening, and hiding there . . . Gérard present, though concealed from view, at the encounter between Juliette Boynet and Monsieur Charles, perhaps witnessing the handing over of a wad of notes, and determined to get possession of them as soon as his aunt was alone. . . .

Very well! In that case, it must be supposed that Gérard, having committed the murder, had spent the rest of the night in the apartment, since the concierge had not let anyone out.

It would therefore follow that Cécile had been intending to name her brother as the murderer when she sat waiting for Maigret in the "aquarium" at the Quai des Orfèvres. . . .

If all this were true, then it must have been Gérard who had lured her into the broom closet.

But how could Gérard Pardon, who had never had any dealings with the police, possibly have known of the existence of that broom closet, let alone of the door connecting the Police Judiciaire building with the Palais de Justice?

A sudden stirring beside him, a skirt being pulled down, the final credits on the screen, all the lights blazing at once, a prolonged tramping of feet.

Maigret, standing in line like everyone else, looked at his neighbor with interest and saw a serene little face, fresh rounded cheeks, and innocently smiling eyes. He had guessed right, the man she was with was in his forties and wore a wedding ring.

Still feeling somewhat dazed, the Chief Superintendent went out into the noisy hubbub of Boulevard Montparnasse. The time, he guessed, was about six. It was growing dark. Shadowy figures hurried past the lighted shop windows. Feeling thirsty, he went into La Coupole, sat down at a table near the window, and ordered a beer.

He was in a state of indolent lassitude, postponing the time when he would have to return to the harsh realities of life. By rights, he ought to be hurrying back to the Quai des Orfèvres, where Lucas was no doubt grappling with his Pole.

Instead, he ordered a ham sandwich and went on gazing dreamily at the passing crowds. Just now in the movie it had taken him a while, as much as a quarter of an hour perhaps, to identify the cause of his uneasiness, namely, the disparity between the lip movements on the screen and the words on the sound track.

How long would it take him to pinpoint the jarring element in the Bourg-la-Reine case? The sandwich was tasty. The beer was good. He ordered another glass.

Almost invariably, when he was engaged on a sensational inquiry, some newspaper or other would print a piece on "The Methods of Chief Superintendent Maigret." It might almost be called a tradition.

Well! Journalists were welcome to their opinions, like anyone else! Maigret came out of the movies. . . . He had a sandwich . . . He drank beer. . . . Sitting beside the steamy window of La Coupole, he might have been a substantial property owner from the provinces, dazzled by the bustle of the streets of Paris.

To tell the truth, his mind was a blank. . . . He was on Boulevard Montparnasse, and yet he was not, because wherever he happened to be, the wedge-shaped house was always right there with him. He was forever going in and out of it. Spying on Madame "Saving-Your-Presence" in her lair. Climbing the stairs and coming down again.

Fact number one: the old woman with dyed hair had been strangled. . . . Fact number two: her money and her papers had disappeared. . . .

Eight hundred thousand francs. . . .

To be precise, eight hundred thousand francs in one-thousand-franc bills. He tried to picture the thickness of such a bundle of bills.

Cécile sitting down to wait in the "aquarium" at the Quai des Orfèvres at eight o'clock in the morning.

It was odd, but he was already having difficulty in recalling her face, distinctive and familiar though it had been. He could see the black coat, the green hat, and the bag on her lap, that enormous ridiculous bag that she was never without, and which looked like a small trunk.

Now Cécile too had been killed, and the bag had vanished.

Maigret sat there, holding up his glass, wholly unaware, needless to say, of what was in it. If anyone had spoken to him just then, he would have had to make a long journey back to the present.

What was it that did not ring true?

He must not go too fast, or the elusive truth might be frightened away before he had time to grasp it.

Cécile . . . the bag . . . the broom closet . . .

The strangled aunt . . .

Because the young woman with the squint had also been strangled, it had been assumed that the two murders . . .

He heaved a sigh of relief and took a deep draught of frothy beer.

Everybody, himself included, had been looking for a single murderer, and that was why they were going around in circles, like a sightless horse on a merry-go-round.

But why not two? He had had vague doubts from the start.

"*L'Intransigeant*, late extra! *L'Intransigeant*, late extra! Read all about it!"

He bought the paper. The picture on the front page caused him to frown. It was of himself, looking fatter than he believed himself to be, biting fiercely on his pipe, with his hand on the shoulder of a young man in a trench coat, who was none other than Gérard. He could not remember having put his hand on Cécile's brother's shoulder. Presumably it had been a reflex action.

The reporter had thought it significant. The caption read as follows:

Does this mean nothing, or can it be that Chief Superintendent Maigret is laying his heavy hand on a cringing murderer?

"Idiot! . . . Waiter! . . . My bill!"

He was furious and yet, at the same time, pleased. He

left La Coupole with a lighter tread than when he had gone in there from the movies. Taxi. What the hell! What if the accounts department did query it on the grounds that the métro was the fastest means of getting from one place to another!

Ten minutes later, he was back at headquarters, absorbing its atmosphere on his way to his office. The Pole was in there, perched awkwardly on the edge of a chair, while Lucas was occupying the Chief Superintendent's own armchair. Maigret winked at Lucas, who, quick to take the hint, went with him into the inspectors' room next door.

"Janvier and I between us have been at him for ten hours now. He's stood up to it so far, but I have the feeling he's beginning to crack.

"My guess is that we won't be through until early tomorrow morning."

The Pole would not be the first to be driven to the wall slowly but surely!

"Now if you could look in yourself, around about two or three, and clinch it. . . ."

"I can't spare the time," grumbled Maigret.

The offices were about to be vacated. One solitary light was kept burning in the vast dusty corridor, and one solitary man was on duty at the switchboard. But in Maigret's office the Pole was still sitting opposite a determined Lucas, who would be relieved by Janvier at intervals, to enable him to slip out for a glass of beer and a bite to eat at the Brasserie Dauphine.

"Any phone calls for me?"

"One from someone called Dandurand."

"Did he leave a message?"

"He said he had something of interest to tell you . . . and that you could reach him at his apartment."

"Any callers?"

"Not that I know of. . . . You'd better ask the guard. . . ."

"A young man in a raincoat, wearing a black armband. He seemed very agitated. He asked me what time you would be back. I told him I couldn't say. He wanted me to give him your home address, but I refused."

"Gérard Pardon?"

"Could be. . . . He refused to fill in a form."

"What time was this?"

"About half an hour ago."

"Did he by any chance have a newspaper with him?" asked the Chief Superintendent, much to the astonishment of the messenger.

"Yes, he did. . . . *L'Intransigeant*. He was holding it all crumpled up in his hand."

Maigret went back to the inspectors' room.

"Anyone free in here? . . . Torrence?"

"I'm due at Bourg-la-Reine, Chief."

"Don't bother about that. I want you to go to Rue du Pas-de-la-Mule. Number Twenty-two. Do you know the boy?"

"Cécile's brother, do you mean? Yes . . . I saw him at Bourg-la . . ."

"Good! I want you to call at his lodgings. I hope he's back there by now. If he's in, don't let him out of your sight . . . I don't want him doing anything foolish, do you understand? . . . Be nice to him . . . I don't want him scared off, quite the reverse."

"What if he isn't there?"

Maigret's brow darkened. He shrugged helplessly.

"If he's not back that would be a disaster. There'll be nothing left but to wait for a phone call from the river police. . . . Unless, by any chance, he's managed to get hold of a gun. . . . Just a minute. . . . You'd better call me in any event at . . . let me think . . . who in the building would be likely to have a telephone? . . . Of course! Dandurand! Call me at Charles Dandurand's apartment. You'll find the number in the directory. Good night, my boy."

He went back into his office for a moment and lingeringly examined the Pole from head to foot, as if to assess his stamina. Then, with another wink to Lucas, this time signifying "He's falling apart!," he left.

He took a taxi to the now familiar building at Bourg-la-Reine. He looked around. Where was the detective who was supposed to be watching the house? A figure loomed out of the shadows.

"Here I am, Chief."

It was Verduret, a new recruit, a pleasant youth, tremendously overawed by the Chief. He could scarcely address him without stammering.

"Any developments?"

"Monsieur Charles, the fourth-floor tenant, came home by streetcar at six o'clock. There was someone waiting for him in the hall. . . . A little fat man in a belted gray overcoat, carrying a briefcase."

It did not take Maigret long to identify this visitor as Monfils's lawyer, Maître Leloup.

"Did he stay long?"

"Half an hour. The Hungarian went out about five, and I haven't seen him since. As for his daughter . . ."

The young inspector waved toward a couple of shadowy figures pressed up against the fence on the patch of waste ground.

"They've been there for the last three quarters of an hour," he said with a sigh. "And they haven't moved in all that time. . . ."

Unseen by the inspector, Maigret blushed, and went into the building. In passing, he waved to Madame Benoit, who was sitting with a plate of soup in front of her, and climbed the four flights of stairs with a heavy tread. Monsieur Charles must have recognized his step, because he opened the door before the Chief Superintendent had time to ring the bell.

"I was expecting you. Do please come in. After your meeting with my friends this morning . . ."

The Chief Superintendent was finding it uncommonly hard to get used to the rancid smell of the old bachelor's flat. He found the atmosphere physically as well as morally repugnant, and he puffed furiously at his pipe, emitting dense clouds of smoke.

"What was the object of Maître Leloup's visit?"

"So you've already heard? . . . He's threatening me with a lawsuit over the estate. He's convinced that Juliette made a will. Apparently, she said as much more than once in letters she wrote to her cousin Monfils, wishing him a happy New Year. . . . I think you ought to make him show them to you. It seems she referred to her nephew and nieces as degenerates and parasites, and complained that, after all she had done for them out of respect for her sister's memory, all they cared about was her money. . . .

" '*They'll get the shock of their lives,*' she wrote in conclusion, '*and so will the Boynets and the Machepieds, when they find out that I have made you my sole heir.*' "

"Did Maître Leloup go no further than to threaten you?"

Monsieur Charles's lips twitched in a chilly smile.

"He made me what he called a fair and generous offer."

"Share and share alike?"

"More or less. If there really were a will, it would be worth considering."

Monsieur Dandurand cracked his finger joints.

"However, that lot didn't know Juliette as I did. To tell the truth, I was the only one who knew her as she really was. She was so terrified of dying, of having one day to leave all her money behind, that she almost persuaded herself that she would never die, at least not in the foreseeable future. She often used to say to me:

" 'When I grow old . . .' "

Much as he disliked the man, Maigret could tell that he was speaking the truth. He himself had never seen Juliette, except as a corpse with crudely dyed hair, yet the impression he had formed of her corresponded exactly with Monsieur Charles's account.

"So?"

"I showed Maître Leloup the door. But it wasn't about that that I called you. I'm well aware that my position is delicate, and I realize that, as far as I'm concerned, the best thing that could happen would be for you to find the killer."

"Or the killers," mumbled Maigret, apparently immersed in contemplation of a water color hanging on the wall.

"Or the . . . ? Well, have it your own way. . . . Come to think of it, for all we know, there might be several killers."

"At any rate, there are two corpses, and, therefore, two murders."

And Maigret placidly relit his pipe.

"It's just a theory. . . . As I was saying, soon after you left, I remembered . . ."

He picked up a clothbound notebook from his desk.

"When you've been in the legal profession as long as I was, you can't easily shed the habits of a lifetime. . . . Every time I paid Juliette the interest on her investments, I was careful to record the numbers of the bills. Perhaps it was foolish of me, but as things have turned out you might find the information useful."

The notebook was filled with figures.

"Remember, I had nothing else to occupy my time."

Maigret could just imagine him in his evil-smelling study, transcribing columns of figures with chill satisfaction. True, the bills hadn't belonged to him. All the same, he had derived a sensuous satisfaction from handling them, recording the numbers, clipping them together into so many bundles, then sorting them into larger bundles, secured with elastic bands.

"I'm sure you won't forget," he concluded, handing the notebook to the Chief Superintendent, "if you collect the reward that my friends have offered to put up, that I gave you every assistance."

They could hear Nouchi bounding up the stairs, three at a time. She paused for a moment on the landing outside. Had she been behaving as improperly as the plump girl in the cinema?

What business was it of the Chief Superintendent's, anyway? In what way could the behavior of this urchin . . . ?

"Well! That's it. . . . Not wishing to be out when you called, I didn't dine at my usual restaurant, but made do with a cold chop at home. Did you have dinner? Can I give you a small glass of something?"

"No, really, thanks . . ."

"Sooner or later, you'll realize that I've done all I could and . . . Oh well! . . . as you please. . . ."

Maigret, without so much as a parting word, opened the door and let in a gust of piano music. This was no doubt old Mademoiselle Paucot's way of compensating for the scales she had to listen to all day long from her pupils.

Four

One day Madame Maigret, who had for some time been contemplating her husband with a very thoughtful look, suddenly gave a sigh and remarked with almost comical candor:

"What surprises me is that more people haven't been goaded into slapping you in your time. . . ."

It was a heartfelt sentiment. For there were times when, even with her, Maigret could be intolerably superior, and his wife was probably the only person to know that he meant nothing by it. It was not that he gave an impression of irony, or twinkled with mischief. It was nothing like that at all. He presented a smooth, impermeable surface, impossible to dent, and whatever anyone else might do, say, or feel had no effect on him whatsoever. Did the Chief Superintendent even hear what you were saying? Did he know that you were there, or could he see nothing but the wall above your head? He was apt to interrupt you in the middle of a sentence with some remark entirely unconnected with what you had been saying.

So now, while Charles Dandurand was still speaking above the piano chords which could be heard through the open door, Maigret stood still, as if listening to the music. How long had he been deaf to what was being said? How far had his mind wandered during those few brief moments? Suddenly, he said:

"You do have a telephone, don't you?"

"Yes . . . of course. . . ."

Was he even aware of the presence of Dandurand, standing there waiting to shut the door behind him? Hesitantly, he murmured to himself:

"I wonder . . ."

It was not intentional, but this habit of his had dismayed and confused others besides the former lawyer. What did he want? What notion had he got hold of now? Was it significant or trivial? There was no way of telling. He was nodding to himself, his heavy eyebrows knitted. At last he murmured:

"Oh! And by the way, I forgot to tell you . . . I gave your name, in case there were any messages for me. . . . Meanwhile, will you please come upstairs with me. If the phone rings, we're bound to hear it up there."

"If you wouldn't mind waiting a moment, I'll just get my key."

On the fifth-floor landing, the Chief Superintendent paused.

"I think you told me that it was shortly after midnight. Were you wearing slippers?"

He looked down at Monsieur Charles's feet, at present clad in brown kid slippers.

"I presume you didn't normally ring the bell."

"Juliette used to wait for me at the door . . . I didn't even have to knock."

"Right! . . . Come on in. . . . Was there a light on in the foyer?"

"No. A lamp was lit in the sitting room, and the door was open."

"One moment . . . I'll switch on the sitting-room light."

"That light wasn't on, Chief Superintendent, only that fake alabaster table lamp over there."

Monsieur Charles, though inwardly uneasy, was pretending to enter into the spirit of the game, as if he hadn't a care in the world.

"As you see," he seemed to be saying, "you can't scare me with your tricks. I have nothing to fear, nothing to hide. On the contrary, I am as anxious as you are to arrive at the truth. If you want to re-enact the events of that night, I will cooperate. . . ."

And aloud he said:

"I should mention that I was wearing this same suit, but with a white scarf instead of a tie.

"I was carrying—sorry, no, I had slipped it into my jacket pocket—an envelope containing . . ."

"Later . . . for the present, if you don't mind, we'll concentrate on tidying up this room. I daresay you know exactly where everything ought to go."

Both men looked very solemn, and Monsieur Charles, with tongue in cheek, was scrupulously careful to put every chair in the correct position, stepping back now and then to get a better view.

"There . . . that's about right."

"Tell me this . . . When Madame Boynet went to the door to let you in, I presume she used her cane?"

"She could barely walk without a cane."

"Can you describe what she was wearing?"

"That's easy. She had on a green flannel dressing gown over her nightdress. I remember noticing that her stockings were bunched around her ankles."

"Both stockings?"

"Yes, both! She usually wore two stockings, if that's what you want to know. And shabby, felt-soled slippers. Juliette took no pride in her appearance. In fact, I think she got some sort of a kick out of looking her worst, and that night she certainly did, with her hair all over the place, her face shiny with cream, and her eyes puffy."

"Did you notice if there were any other lights on in the apartment? You say you never left this room?"

"That is correct."

"Where was Madame Boynet sitting?"

"At her desk, which she proceeded to open. She knew that I had come to settle accounts with her."

"One moment. . . . Where did she get the key from?"

At this, the lawyer seemed momentarily nonplused.

"I . . . as a matter of fact, I don't recall . . . I think she must have had it in the pocket of her dressing gown."

"Come now, Monsieur Dandurand. . . . Her reason for opening the desk when you were about to discuss money matters must have been to refer to the relevant papers."

"Obviously . . ."

Monsieur Charles, suddenly looking grave, reflected.

"You're right . . . I must admit it hadn't struck me . . ."

"What did you talk about all this time?"

"We never talked much . . . I think I mentioned that I felt a cold coming on, to explain why I was wearing a scarf. . . . I also told her that it would probably be necessary for me to go to Béziers."

Maigret's glance swept the room. His next question seemed even more irrelevant.

"Were all the clocks going?"

Some of them had stopped by now, and the Chief Superintendent, scarcely aware of what he was doing, began winding them up. They did not all show the same time.

"I didn't notice."

What could it possibly matter, anyway?

"You will observe, Monsieur Dandurand, that although Mademoiselle Paucot's apartment is three floors beneath us, we can hear her piano almost as clearly as from your apartment. Sound carries in this building . . . which is just as well, as I can't fail to hear your telephone if anyone calls me at your number. . . . To proceed. . . . Were you sitting where you are now? . . . Now, about that envelope you mentioned, containing . . ."

"Fifty-two thousand francs . . . the quarterly rents from the house on Rue d'Antin. . . ."

"Did she count the bills?"

"She invariably did."

"Did she know you kept a note of the numbers?"

"I never told her. . . . While she was pinning the thousand-franc bills together in bundles of ten, I drew her attention to the fact that lately we had not been getting any replies to our letters addressed to the establishment at Béziers. The woman we had put in charge there, and who . . ."

He looked at Maigret. The Chief Superintendent, it seemed to him, was not listening, and, what was more, he evidently attached no importance to what he was saying. Smoking his pipe, Maigret gazed from one to another of the family photographs. Those of the three children especially seemed to interest him. Then his eyes fixed on another photograph, the only studio portrait in the apartment, of a voluptuous young woman of about thirty, with provocative eyes and breasts. A fine-looking woman, in fact, and none other than Juliette herself.

"Go on, Monsieur Dandurand."

"In our sort of business, it's difficult if not impossible to exercise direct control, and, as we have already explained, where irregularities occur, one has no legal redress. Which explains why . . ."

Maigret went and opened the dining-room door, and then shut it again.

"Go on, go on. . . . Pay no attention to me. . . ."

Dandurand, somewhat disconcerted, talked on as best he could, and this time Maigret even walked out of the room.

"I suggested going to Béziers to look into things myself. . . . It seemed to me that the only way of ascertaining the average receipts was to talk to the girls. . . ."

"Go on," persisted the Chief Superintendent, from a distance.

"As you wish. . . . I remember remarking that the drop in income—it had fallen by a third in the last month—could not be attributed solely to the fact that it was the off season, and . . ."

Eventually, the Chief Superintendent reappeared in the doorway. He looked at Monsieur Charles in some bewilderment, as if to say:

What does this fellow think he is doing here, and talking to himself too!

"Tell me . . . while you were discussing these matters, you didn't happen to hear any sounds in the apartment, did you? Were you making any effort to keep your voice down?"

"I was talking very quietly. Juliette was always afraid of waking her niece, even though she was sedated. She was also mistrustful of the Hungarians next door, whom she could hear shouting and quarreling all day long. She'd been trying to get rid of them for months, but they resorted to every means in their power to thwart her."

"What did she do with the fifty-two thousand francs?"

"She still had them in her hand when she saw me out. . . ."

"In the envelope?"

"I think she had put the notes back in the envelope, yes . . ."

"What sort of envelope?"

"Just an old envelope I had in my desk. . . . Let me think. . . . It was buff-colored. . . . What letters did I get that day? Yes! I'm almost sure it was a Crédit Lyonnais envelope, with my name and address typed on it."

"Did you ever see the envelope again?"

"Never."

He could not help sounding faintly contemptuous. Did Maigret really think he could impress him with all this twaddle?

"Do you mind if I smoke, Chief Superintendent?"

"Ah! That reminds me. When you used to call on your friend Juliette, did you ever smoke in here?"

"Often."

"Cigarettes, or what?"

"I see you are better informed than I had supposed, and if I had anything on my conscience . . . But how did you know? I understood that you had never seen Juliette alive. . . ."

This time, if not actually worried, he could not help being intrigued.

"Well . . . there are no ashtrays in this room. I'm quite sure I never left any cigarette butts lying about. As to the ash . . ."

He laughed uneasily.

"To tell you the truth, Chief Superintendent, I don't understand. I'll tell you the whole story, and then you'll see why I'm so puzzled. Once, many years ago, I came in here smoking my pipe. Now Juliette was a woman with strong views of her own, and she disapproved of pipe smoking in the presence of a woman. But then some nights it took us several hours to get through our business, so I got into the habit of bringing a package of cigarettes up with me. Not wishing to drop ash all over the place, I would spread a piece of paper on the corner of the desk and use it as an ashtray, and I would take it away with me when I left . . ."

Maigret's abstracted expression did not change.

"How you could possibly know? That really is . . . unless . . ."

"Unless what?" echoed the Chief Superintendent.

"Unless there was someone hidden in the apartment, spying on everything we said and did. . . . And even then, it would have had to be someone who had access to you, and could tell you . . ."

"What does it matter? When Juliette Boynet saw you to the door, she had the fifty-two thousand francs in her hand. . . . As to the envelope, you probably used it for your cigarette ash. . . . Juliette locked the door behind you, I take it?"

"She bolted it."

"Did you go straight back to your apartment? Did you see anyone on the way? Did you hear anything? I suppose you can't tell me whether the old woman went straight to bed?"

"I don't know. . . ."

They listened. The insistent ringing of a bell was clearly to be heard. Maigret went to the door, muttering:

"Excuse me. . . . That must be the phone call I've been waiting for. . . ."

The door to the fourth-floor apartment had been left ajar. The lights were on. The telephone stood on the desk.

"Hello! . . . Torrence?"

"Is that you, Chief? I'm still at Rue du Pas-de-la-Mule. . . ."

"And Gérard?"

"I haven't seen him. Listen . . . It's a bit involved . . . I don't think I ought to say too much on the telephone . . ."

"Hold on a minute."

The inspector wondered what was going on. The fact was that Maigret could hear footsteps just above his head. The sound, he reckoned, must be coming from Juliette Boynet's bedroom. He could hear it distinctly. Monsieur Charles's felt-shod feet and stealth were to no avail. His comings and goings were plainly audible.

Thus, it was obvious that the former lawyer could hear from his study everything that went on in the apartment on the floor above.

"Hello! . . . Are you still there, Chief?"

"Shut up!"

"Shall I hold on?"

"I said shut up!"

Suddenly, leaving the receiver lying on the desk, he made a dash for the floor above. When he opened the door of Madame Boynet's apartment, Monsieur Charles, looking somber but impassive, seemed on the way to come out.

"Was it the call you were expecting?"

"Yes, I haven't quite finished yet. If you'd care to come down . . ."

"Sorry . . . I didn't want to intrude."

Maigret intercepted what appeared to be a look of chagrin, if not anguish, in the eyes of this hitherto cool customer.

"I'm coming, Chief Superintendent. . . . If I'd known that . . ."

"You go first."

"Where are we going?"

"Into your study. Shut the door. Stay where you are, and, if you don't mind, keep your hands on the table."

He picked up the receiver again.

"I'm listening . . ."

"Ah! I thought we'd been cut off. . . . Well, Chief, here goes. . . . When I got here I inquired of the concierge, and she told me that Gérard Pardon hadn't come in yet but that his wife was at home. . . . I went and stood guard near the front door. And then it began to rain."

"Never mind that."

"I'm soaked through! Oh, hell! . . . I didn't dare pop into the café on the corner for a drop of something. I stood there for hours. . . . And then, just now, within the last quarter of an hour, a young woman arrived in a taxi. She looked worried. I recognized her by her red hat as Gérard's sister, Mademoiselle Berthe, the one you pointed out to me."

"Go on. . . ."

Little did he know, as he made his report, that the Chief Superintendent was listening with only half an ear, while his eyes were fixed on Monsieur Charles, whom he was inspecting from head to foot. As to the former lawyer, he was making no secret of the awkwardness of having to stand there with both hands flat on the desk.

What had he been doing up there? It was the first time since Juliette's death that he had had a few minutes to himself in her apartment.

"Go on . . . I'm listening."

"I had no instructions. The girl went upstairs. . . . After a while, it occurred to me that she might be the bearer of bad news, so I went up after her. I knocked at the door. She was the one who let me in. There's no foyer . . . Madame Pardon was in the kitchen, sobbing. She looked at me in terror, and gasped:

" *'Is he dead?'* "

Monsieur Charles must have caught a look of astonishment on Maigret's face. He frowned.

"What then . . . ?"

"It was very embarrassing, I can tell you, Chief. . . . I asked the girl what she had come for. She replied that we were a heartless bunch, and that if anything had happened to her brother, she would hold us responsible. . . . Well, what with one of them in tears and the other in a rage, I couldn't get any sense out of either of them!

"So I could see that there was nothing for it but to be patient, and in the end I gathered that Gérard had been to see his sister. . . . Apparently, he was behaving like a madman. . . . He wanted money, and he wanted it at once.

"She tried to calm him down, and asked him what he wanted the money for. . . .

"He replied with a spiteful laugh:

" 'You'll find out when you see tomorrow's papers. . . . For God's sake, give me all you can spare.'

"And she gave him exactly a hundred and thirty francs, leaving herself with only ten francs. He made a wild dash for the door. She tried to follow him, but he leaped onto a moving bus. . . .

"I don't know what to do next, Chief. . . . I had to leave them to telephone. . . . Should I go back there? Gérard's wife says he means to kill himself. If you ask me, I . . ."

"Fine!" said Maigret, cutting him off in mid-sentence.

"But . . . what am I to do now?"

But the Chief Superintendent had already hung up, and, without a pause, he ordered Monsieur Charles to empty his pockets.

"You want me to . . . ?"

"Empty your pockets!"

"If you say so . . ."

Slowly, he did so, taking things out one by one and laying them on the table: a shabby wallet, a key, a pen-knife, an exceedingly grubby handkerchief, various papers, a small box of cough lozenges, a tobacco pouch, a pipe, and a box of matches.

"Turn your pockets inside out. . . . Take off your jacket. . . ."

"Do you want me to strip?"

If Madame Maigret had been there, she might have been tempted to repeat the remark, suitably amended, which she had made to her husband:

"What surprises me is that you haven't been goaded into slapping him!"

And indeed, of the two, it was Monsieur Charles who was the more impassive, the more chilly, with a coolness verging on insolence. He took off his jacket, to reveal a shirt with frayed grayish cuffs. His waistcoat was passable. His braces were in no better condition than his shirt, and the waistband of his underpants showed above his trousers.

"Shall I carry on?"

If the Chief Superintendent had not exercised considerable self-control, he would have done more than slap the fellow, he would have driven his fist into his face.

"Do you want me to take off my slippers?"

"Yes."

This exercise revealed no hidden scrap of paper, only a hole in one sock.

"I might point out. Chief Superintendent, that it is eleven o'clock at night, and that even if you had a warrant, properly drawn up and duly signed, I should be entitled to show you the door at this hour. . . . Not that I would think of doing such a thing. I just want to draw your attention . . ."

"Sit down."

He dialed a number.

"Make yourself at home!" murmured the former lawyer sarcastically.

"Hello! . . . Put me through to Lucas, will you? Is that you? . . . Not yet? . . . Keep at it, my boy. . . . No! I can't spare the time. . . . Whom have you got there? . . . Berger? . . . Oh, very well! . . . Tell him to hop into a taxi and come to Bourg-la-Reine. . . . Yes. . . . Fourth floor. . . . Thanks. . . . Good luck!"

He hung up and remained motionless, staring down at the desk in front of him.

"If you're staying, perhaps you'd care to join me in a drink?"

Maigret quelled him with a look. Ten minutes went by, a quarter of an hour. Cars roared past on the Route Nationale. The piano was silent. The whole house slept.

At last, downstairs, there could be heard the slam of the front door, followed by footsteps on the stairs.

"Come in, Berger."

It must have been pouring outside, because, though he had come by taxi, the inspector's hat and shoulders were wet.

"Let me introduce you to Monsieur Charles. . . . He is

rather on edge tonight, and I'm afraid he might do something foolish. . . . I pointed out to him that we have no legal right to spend the night in his apartment, but he doesn't mind! I will leave him in your charge. He's welcome to go to bed if he so wishes, and if he does, be sure you look after him as if he were your nearest and dearest. Understood? I'll probably look in tomorrow morning. Don't worry if I'm a bit late, but don't let him out. He might catch cold."

He buttoned up his coat and filled his pipe, gently pressing down the tobacco with his thumb.

"I'd keep off his brandy, if I were you. I would think it isn't up to much."

He picked up the wallet and papers that Dandurand had taken from his pockets.

"Did you tell the taxi to wait?"

"No, Chief."

"Never mind. Good night."

And he left the two men alone together. He considered going back up to the fifth floor, but thought better of it. Dandurand was not the man to leave incriminating evidence lying about.

Madame "Saving-Your-Presence," in her night attire, was waiting for him in the hall downstairs. Her head was twisted even farther to one side than usual.

"What's going on, Chief Superintendent? Has there been another murder in the house?"

He was not listening. He could barely make out the whispered words, and he replied absently:

"Maybe. . . . Let me out, please."

Part Three

One

It was still raining the following morning. The rain was soft, cheerless and hopeless, like a widow's tears. It could be felt rather than seen, although it spread over everything like a cold layer of varnish and dotted the Seine with countless little vibrant circles. Those starting out for work as late as nine o'clock might well have imagined that they were in time to catch the milk train, with the gas lamps still alight in the lingering darkness.

Maigret, as he reached the top of the stairs at police headquarters, glanced involuntarily at the "aquarium" and could not shake off the feeling that he would see Cécile sitting there in her usual place, humble and resigned, as she had been on her last visit. An ugly thought had formed in his mind this morning, he could not imagine why. No doubt, as he walked along half asleep, sheltering close to the walls of the dripping houses, the girl in the movie house, Nouchi, and Monsieur Charles had flitted like shadows across his consciousness. And now, in the corridor leading to his office, it occurred to him to wonder whether Cécile and Monsieur Dandurand . . .

He had no grounds for any such suspicion. It was distasteful to him. It sullied his recollections, and yet the Chief Superintendent's thoughts kept reverting to it.

"Wait a minute . . . There's someone . . . The Chief Commissioner would like to see you at once."

It was the guard, who was preventing Maigret from going into his own office.

"Did you say there was someone in there?" he asked.

A minute or so later, he was knocking at the Chief Commissioner's door.

"Come in, Maigret. Feeling better? Look, I've taken the liberty of using your office as a waiting room for a visitor. I couldn't think where else to put him. Besides, it's your pigeon, really. Here, read this."

Maigret stared blankly at the proffered visiting card, which read:

JEAN TINCHANT

Minister of State at the Foreign Office
begs the Chief Commissioner of the Police Judiciaire to give every assistance to Monsieur Spencer Oats of the Institute of Criminology of Philadelphia, who has been highly recommended to us by the United States Embassy

"What does he want?"

"To study your methods."

And the Chief Commissioner could not help laughing as he watched Maigret stride away, with shoulders hunched and fists clenched, for all the world as if he were bent on pounding the American criminologist to a pulp.

"I'm delighted to meet you, Chief Superintendent. . . ."

"One moment, Monsieur Spencer. . . . Hello! . . . Switchboard? . . . Maigret speaking. Any messages for me? . . . He hasn't been found yet? . . . Get me Bourg-la-Reine nineteen . . ."

Quite a likable fellow, this American. A tall, scholarly-looking young man, with red hair and a thin face, wearing a sober suit of good cut, and speaking with a slight, rather pleasant accent.

"Is that you, Berger? . . . Well? . . ."

"Nothing, Chief. . . . He bedded down on the divan, fully dressed. I must say I'm feeling hungry, and there isn't a thing to eat in the flat. I daren't take the risk of slipping out to buy some croissants. Will you be coming soon? . . . No! He's as good as gold. He even went so far as to say he didn't blame you, and that he'd have done the same in your place. . . . He's quite confident that you will soon realize you have made a mistake."

Maigret hung up and went across to his stove, which he proceeded to light, much to the surprise of the American.

"What can I do for you, Monsieur Spencer?"

He deliberately chose to call him by his Christian name because he had not the least idea how to pronounce Oats.

"To begin with, Chief Superintendent, I should very much like to hear your views on the psychology of the murderer. . . ."

Maigret, meanwhile, had picked up his mail from his desk and was opening it.

"Which murderer?" he asked, glancing through his letters.

"Why . . . murderers in general."

"*Before* or *after*?"

"What do you mean?"

Maigret smoked his pipe, read his letters, warmed his back, and seemed to attach no importance to this disjointed interchange.

"What I mean is, are you referring to murderers *before* or *after* they have committed the crime? Because, needless to say, *before* they are not yet murderers. . . . For thirty, forty, fifty years of their lives, longer sometimes, they are just people like anyone else, aren't they?"

"Of course. . . ."

At long last, Maigret looked up and, with a mischievous twinkle in his eye, said:

"What makes you think, Monsieur Spencer, that just killing one of his own kind should change a man's character from one minute to the next?"

He went over to the window and gazed out at the little circles on the Seine.

"So what it really comes down to," said the American, "is that a murderer is a man like any other. . . ."

There was a knock on the door. Lucas came in, carrying a file of papers. Catching sight of the visitor, he seemed about to beat a retreat.

"What is it, my boy? Ah! Yes. . . . Well then, you'd better take the file across to the D.P.P.'s office . . . I take it the Hôtel des Arcades is still under surveillance?"

Lucas brought him up to date on the Polish case, but Maigret had not lost the thread of his argument.

"Why does a man commit murder, Monsieur Spencer? From motives of jealousy, greed, hatred, envy; sometimes, though more rarely, from necessity. . . . In other words, he may be driven by any one of the human passions. . . . Now every one of us is subject to these passions to a greater or lesser degree. My neighbor invariably opens his window on summer nights and blows his hunting horn. Consequently, I hate him. But I very much doubt if I shall murder him. . . . And yet, only last month, a retired colonial servant, whose temper had been shortened by recurring bouts of tropical fever, fired a shot at the man who lived in the apartment above him, because he had a wooden leg and would insist on pacing up and down all night, pounding the floorboards."

"I can see what you mean. . . . But what about the psychology of the murderer *afterward*?"

"That's no concern of mine. . . . That's a matter for juries and prison governors and guards. . . . My job is to find the culprit. And for that purpose, all that concerns me is his personality *before* the act. Whether he had it in him to commit that particular murder, and how and when he committed it. . . ."

"The Chief Commissioner gave me to understand that you might perhaps allow me to be present at . . ."

He wouldn't be the first! So much the worse for him!

"I know you are working on the Bourg-la-Reine case,

and I have followed the newspaper reports with great interest. . . . Do you know already who did it?"

"I know who didn't, at any rate. . . . All the same, he . . . Allow me to ask you a question, Monsieur Spencer. A man believes himself to be a suspect. Rightly or wrongly, he imagines the police are in possession of evidence incriminating him. His wife is expecting a child at any moment. There isn't so much as a penny in the house. . . . This man rampages into his sister's flat like a madman, demanding money, every penny she's got. His sister gives him a hundred and thirty francs. . . . What does he do with it?"

And Maigret pushed a newspaper across the desk to his visitor. It was the evening paper of the previous day, with the photograph of Maigret laying his hand on Gérard Pardon's shoulder.

"Is this the young man?"

"That's him. . . . Last night, from this office, I broadcast his description to all police stations up and down the country. A watch is being kept on all frontiers. . . . A hundred and thirty francs . . ."

"Are you saying he's innocent?"

"I am convinced that he is not guilty of the murder of either his aunt or his sister. . . . If he had asked for the money earlier in the day, I would have concluded that he wanted it to buy a revolver to shoot himself."

"But he's innocent?"

"Precisely, Monsieur Spencer . . . that's the point I'm trying to make. An innocent man may have the seeds of guilt in him, just as a guilty man may be innocent at heart. . . . Luckily, by the time the boy got hold of the hundred and thirty francs, the gunsmiths had already put up their shutters. I presume, therefore, that he's on the run. . . . So the question is, how far could he go with a hundred and thirty francs? . . . Just about across the Belgian frontier. . . ."

He picked up the receiver and asked to be put through to the Forensic Laboratory.

"Hello! . . . Maigret here. . . . Who is that speaking? Oh, it's you, Jaminet! I want you to get your gear together and rustle up an assistant. . . . Yes. . . . And wait for me downstairs in a taxi."

Then, turning to the American:

"We may be about to make an arrest."

"You know who did it?"

"I think so, but I'm not sure. . . . To tell the truth, I'd be inclined to . . . Would you mind waiting for me here for a few minutes, Monsieur Spencer?"

Maigret went through to the Palais de Justice, making use of the notorious communicating door which should have been bricked up years ago, that same door without which Cécile could not have died where she did. It was so convenient! What good had it done to repeat, year after year, for the past ten or was it twenty years . . . ?

The Chief Superintendent knocked at the Examining Magistrate's door, but, when invited to take a seat, shook his head.

"I can't stay . . . I've got someone waiting for me. . . . What I came for, Judge, was to ask if you wouldn't mind too much if I were to arrest a man who may turn out to be innocent. I should point out, mind you, that he's a nasty type, with a number of convictions for sexual offenses, and he'd scarcely have the nerve to lodge a complaint."

"In that case . . . What's his name?"

"Charles Dandurand."

Ten minutes later, Maigret and Spencer Oats got into the taxi on the Quai des Orfèvres in which the two technicians from the Forensic Laboratory were waiting. It was shortly after ten when the taxi drew up at Bourg-la-Reine. Juliette Boynet's house was shrouded in a Scotch mist, so that it looked blurred and much faded, as in an old photograph.

"Wait for me upstairs on the fifth-floor landing," said Maigret to the technicians.

He rang Dandurand's bell. Berger, who had dark rings under his eyes from lack of sleep, came to the door.

"Haven't you brought any food?"

Monsieur Charles had taken off his collar. He had the crumpled look of a man who has slept in his clothes. He was wearing a pair of old bedroom slippers.

"I presume . . ." he began.

"I shouldn't presume anything if I were you, Monsieur Dandurand. You're almost sure to get it wrong. I have here a warrant for your arrest, duly signed by the examining magistrate assigned to the case."

"Ah!"

"You don't sound surprised . . ."

"No . . . I'm sorry for you, that's all."

"Have you nothing to say before you leave? You will be kept in custody at the Santé . . ."

"All I have to say is that you are making a mistake."

"Aren't you forgetting what you did yesterday in Juliette Boynet's bedroom, while I was on the telephone in here?"

A bitter smile flickered over the unshaven face of the man.

"Stay with him, Berger. . . . See that he gets dressed. When he's ready, take him to the Préfecture and book him."

Abruptly, he turned around, seized the kid by her thin shoulders, and said angrily:

"Listen to me, Nouchi, if you get under my feet just once more . . ."

"What will you do to me?" she asked, thrilled.

"You'll see, and it will be no joke! . . . Be off with you!"

He went upstairs and proceeded to open the door of the fifth-floor apartment.

"Now, this is what I want you fellows to do . . . Careful, Monsieur Spencer, don't go in there. . . ."

"But we've already fingerprinted the whole apartment," objected the photographer.

"On the day after the murder. Quite right. . . . And only two sets of prints were found in Juliette Boynet's bedroom, her own and Cécile's. There were no men's fingerprints, none of Gérard Pardon's, and none of that sorry rogue's downstairs. . . . But it so happens that last night, while I was speaking on the phone in his study, he came into this room. I'm sure of that because I could hear his footsteps. . . . I don't know what he was up to . . . but he was taking a grave risk, so he must have had some very compelling reason. I want you to find out what he touched . . . so get going! Now do you see why I asked you not to go into that room, Monsieur Spencer?"

The technicians had set up their apparatus, and were getting down to the job. Maigret, his hands in his pockets, wandered from room to room.

"It's not a very pretty story, is it? A miserly, crazy old woman . . . a girl, or rather a somewhat faded young woman, none too generously endowed by nature. Will you come downstairs for a moment?"

They reached Monsieur Charles's apartment just as he was leaving, wearing a hat and coat, in company with Inspector Berger.

"Don't worry about your things, Monsieur Dandurand. I'll take charge of the key to your apartment. Incidentally, you will presumably be appointing a lawyer very shortly to represent you. I shall expect to see him here."

Whereupon he shut the door and went not into the study of the former lawyer but into his bedroom.

"Take a seat, Monsieur Spencer. . . . Listen . . ."

"You can hear every word that's said up there."

"Correct! I don't know what your new houses are like in America, but ours are about as soundproof as cigar boxes. . . . Pay no attention to their footsteps. See if you can make out what they're doing. . . ."

"It sounds as if . . . that's odd. It's much more difficult . . ."

"I agree with you. . . . There, now! Someone is fiddling with a drawer. . . . He's opening it. . . . But can you tell which drawer it is?"

"It's not possible . . ."

"Right! That settles one point. From his own apartment, Dandurand could hear every word that was spoken on the floor above. He could judge more or less where everyone in Juliette Boynet's household happened to be at any given time. On the other hand, the precise details of who was doing what . . . I only hope that idiot Gérard hasn't thrown himself into the Seine!"

"But you say he's innocent!"

"I said I believed he was. . . . Unfortunately, I'm not infallible. . . . I also pointed out that innocent people often behave as if they were guilty. . . . I hope Berthe is still with his wife. At any moment she may give birth to a bouncing boy."

Above their heads, furniture was being dragged across the floor.

"If you were a miser, Monsieur Spencer . . ."

"There are no misers in the States. . . . Miserliness is a characteristic of a mature civilization. We haven't reached that stage yet."

"In that case, let us suppose that you are an old woman, an old Frenchwoman. . . . You are in possession of millions, and yet your life style is no more lavish than that of any widow living on a small, fixed income. . . ."

"I find that difficult to imagine . . ."

"Make an effort. Your only pleasure in life is counting the bills that represent your life savings. That is the problem that has haunted me for the past three days, because, you see, a man's life depends upon it. Find where the money is hidden and you find the killer."

"I suppose . . ." began the American.

"You suppose what?" interrupted Maigret, almost aggressively.

"If I were such a person as you have described . . . I would keep my money where I could readily lay my hands on it at all times."

"That's exactly what I thought . . . but wait! Although considerably handicapped, Juliette Boynet was nevertheless able to get around in the apartment. She would stay in bed in the mornings until about ten, when her niece would bring in her breakfast and the morning paper."

"Maybe she hid the money in her bed? I seem to have heard somewhere that it's common practice in France to sew one's savings into one's mattress."

"The only thing is that, for the rest of the day, until she returned to bed at night, Juliette spent her time in the sitting room. . . . Just before she died, she had eight hundred thousand francs in the house, in thousand-franc bills. That many bills would be quite bulky. Now, listen carefully. There are only two people who could have known where that money was hidden. The old woman's niece, Cécile, who lived with her. She was not in her aunt's confidence, but she might accidentally have . . ."

"Monsieur Dandurand, on the other hand, was in the old lady's confidence, wasn't he?"

"Only to some extent. . . . You can take it from me, he didn't know where she kept the money. Women like Juliette Boynet don't trust anybody, not even their guardian angels! Still, as you yourself have noticed, you can't make a sound up there that isn't heard in this room. . . . Let's go up, shall we? If the telephone rings, we shall hear it."

It was such a humid day that the banister rail was sticky to the touch. In the piano teacher's apartment, a pupil was playing scales. The Hungarians were quarreling, and Nouchi's shrill voice was clearly to be heard.

"Well, boys?"

"It's amazing, Chief . . ."

"What is?"

"Are you sure the fellow wasn't wearing rubber gloves?"

"I know for certain he wasn't."

"He walked on the carpet. . . . But up to now, we haven't found any sign that he touched anything, apart from the door knob. In fact, the only prints we've found are yours."

A powerful spotlight had been plugged into the outlet. The presence of cameras gave a different feel to the room which Juliette Boynet had occupied for so many years.

"She used a cane, didn't she?" the American asked suddenly.

Maigret whipped around as if he had been stung.

"Wait . . . The thing that . . ."

What was the one thing that the old woman could take with her everywhere, from her bedroom into the sitting room and from there into the dining room at mealtimes? Her cane, of course! But it would not be possible to hide eight hundred thousand francs in thousand-franc bills in a cane, even if it were hollow!

The Chief Superintendent took another searching look at the contents of the room.

"What about this?" he asked suddenly, pointing to a small, low, boxlike object, covered in worn tapestry, which Juliette Boynet had probably used as a footstool. "Any prints?"

"Not a thing, Chief."

Maigret picked it up and put it on the bed. He felt along the row of brass studs securing the tapestry, and was able to raise the top, which formed a kind of lid. The interior was lined with a copper receptacle, and had obviously been intended originally as a foot warmer, to be filled with charcoal.

There was a silence. Everyone was staring at a parcel, wrapped in an old newspaper, which was wedged into the copper liner.

"The eight hundred bills must be in here," said Maigret at last, relighting his pipe. "Look, Monsieur Spencer . . . And please don't mention this to your colleagues at the Institute of Criminology, it would be too embarrassing. I had the mattress ripped open and the boxspring taken apart, I had the walls tapped, and the floorboards and the fireplace. And it never occurred to me that an old woman with swollen legs, having to hobble about on a cane, might have this footling little bit of furniture taken from room to room to rest her feet on. Careful with that newspaper! You fellows had better give it a thorough going-over. . . ."

Maigret, wrapped in his own thoughts, spent the next ten minutes setting all the clocks right, as a result of which they all chimed one after another.

"We're done, Chief."

"Are his prints on it?"

"They are. . . . As for the bills, there are eight hundred and ten of them."

"I shall need envelopes and sealing wax."

When the whole of the little fortune was safely under seal, he telephoned the Public Prosecutor's office and arranged for a senior official to come and collect it.

"Will you come with me, Monsieur Spencer?"

Outside in the street, he turned up the collar of his overcoat.

"It's a pity we didn't keep the taxi. . . . But believe it or not, if I'm terrified of anyone, it's those fellows in our accounts department. I don't know if they're as ferocious over expenses in the United States. . . . How about dropping into that bistro over there for a glass of something, while we're waiting for our streetcar? It's where all the local workmen eat. . . . But you've left your hat behind!"

"I never wear a hat."

The Chief Superintendent stared hard at the shock of red hair spattered with glistening beads of rain. There were no two ways about it, some things Maigret would never understand!

"I'll have a Calvados. What about you?"

"Would they have such a thing as a glass of milk, I wonder?"

Maybe that explained how a man of thirty-five had managed to retain a complexion as rosy as the muzzle of a young calf.

"A large glass, barman!"

"Of milk?"

"No! Of Calvados!"

Painstakingly, Maigret pushed fresh tobacco into the bowl of his pipe. Had that cold-blooded scoundrel Dandurand returned the eight hundred thousand francs to their hiding place in the old woman's footstool, and thereby put his life in jeopardy?

Two

The two men had just left the office of the registrar. At first, Maigret's inquiries had been met with a curt refusal to divulge information from a clerk with bad teeth. When the Chief Superintendent had produced his badge, however, the man had responded with such feverish zeal that it had taken him twice as long as necessary to search through the bulky volumes of the register.

The town hall was neither old nor new. It was ugly, ugly as a whole, ugly in every part, ugly in its proportions and in the materials used in its construction. The clock was just striking twelve when Maigret and his American friend, along with most of the town-hall staff, emerged from the building. The gentleman with the bulging stomach, three chins, and slovenly appearance whom everyone treated with deference was presumably none other than the mayor of Bourg-la-Reine.

The Chief Superintendent and his companion stood for a moment at the top of the four or five steps leading up to the portico, waiting for a lull in the heavy downpour of rain. In the little square, sheltered by skeleton trees, the market was packing up. The stalls were being dismantled. The slimy ground was littered with rubbish. Opposite was a butcher's shop, stained with blood from the carcasses. A fat, rosy-cheeked woman could be seen behind the cash counter. Children from a nearby school were being let out for their midday break. They scampered about, shrieking. Many of them were wearing shoes with wooden soles. A green-and-white bus went by. . . .

The atmosphere was neither that of the metropolis, nor that of a small provincial town or village. Maigret stole a glance at the American, and their eyes met. Spencer Oats seemed to read his thoughts, because his mouth twitched in a faint smile. In the rain, his face appeared a little veiled, like the scene before them.

"We have dreary places like this at home as well," he murmured.

The inquiries they had just completed at the town hall could have been entrusted to the most lowly inspector, or indeed to a policeman of the lowest rank. First of all, Maigret had wanted to find out how long Charles Dandurand had lived in his present apartment as a tenant of Juliette Boynet.

He had been there just fourteen years. Before that, he had occupied a furnished apartment on Rue Delambre, near Boulevard Montparnasse.

And the contractor Boynet, Juliette's late husband, had died six months before Dandurand moved in.

The two men, sheltering in the porch of the building, were waiting for the rain to subside.

"Tell me, Monsieur Spencer, do you know why criminals prefer to have dealings with one of us rather than an examining magistrate?"

"I think I'm beginning to get an inkling. . . ."

"I don't deny that we play it rough at times. Less so than is generally supposed, but much more so than any Examining Magistrate or Public Prosecutor's deputy. . . . On the other hand, it is impossible to conduct a police inquiry without, to some extent, entering into the life of the accused. . . . We visit him in his home. . . . We become familiar with his house, his habits, his family, and his friends. . . . This morning I drew a distinction between the murderer *before* and *after* . . . well then, you could say that all our efforts are directed toward getting to know the murderer as he was *before*. . . . Once we hand him over to the Examining Magistrate, our work is done. . . . All connection with his former life as an ordinary man is severed, usually forever. . . . He is a criminal and nothing but a criminal, and is treated as such by the judiciary."

And, without a pause, Maigret went on with a sigh:

"I'd give a lot to know what Charles Dandurand was doing in Juliette's bedroom. . . . Was he putting the bills back in the footstool or . . . ? It seems to be clearing up a little."

They emerged from the shelter of the porch, the Chief Superintendent with his shoulders hunched and his hands in his pockets, the American as unconcerned as if the sun were shining.

"Would you mind having lunch at a bistro?"

"On the contrary, I should be delighted. So far, I have been shepherded about by the officials of my Embassy, and have eaten only in the smartest restaurants."

They took a streetcar to the Porte d'Orléans, going past the wedge-shaped house, its bricks darkened by the rain.

"The problem is to be able to put oneself in their place, to think and feel as they do. This is even harder for a judge, whose life is of necessity remote. . . . The apartment house where I live isn't so very different from this one. . . . Here we are!"

The restaurant chosen by Maigret was in a little side street. It had no frills, just a zinc counter, a few marble-topped tables, and sawdust on the floor. The proprietor, a pleasant man with a florid, somewhat blotchy complexion, wearing a blue denim apron, came and shook hands with the Chief Superintendent.

"It's ages since you last came to see us! Wait till my old woman hears about this! . . . Mélanie! What have you got that's special for Monsieur Maigret?"

Mélanie, pot-bellied, wiping her hands on her apron, emerged from the kitchen.

"If only you'd called to say you were coming . . . Oh, well, never mind! . . . There's *coq au vin*, and some quite good *cèpes*, fresh from the country this morning. . . . I hope your friend likes *cèpes*?"

The place was empty, except for a few regulars. The windows were so steamed up that it was impossible to see out of them.

"Your usual Beaujolais, Monsieur Maigret?"

Maigret went to make a telephone call. The American watched him through the glass panes of the cramped little booth as he dialed the number, looking grave and preoccupied.

"That idiot Gérard hasn't been found yet," he said when he returned to their table. "I'll look in on his wife tonight."

"I think you mentioned that they are hard up?"

"That has been attended to, of course. I wonder if that child will ever learn of the circumstances surrounding its birth. . . . But what I should dearly like to know is why the hell Charles Dandurand . . ."

Whatever else he might talk about, it was plain that he was obsessed with this one question.

"Why did Dandurand . . . ?"

"If he killed the old lady . . ." ventured Spencer Oats.

"If he killed the old lady, then I'm a bigger fool than you take me for, Monsieur Spencer, and I'll have to start the whole inquiry again from scratch. . . . To begin with, why should he have killed her? She was worth more to him alive than dead. . . . He knew he could expect nothing from her heirs. . . . As for stealing the eight hundred thousand francs from her apartment, you saw for yourself that he didn't.

"And besides, how could he have done it? She indicated that their interview was at an end. . . . She saw him to the door. . . . And I'm quite sure she locked it carefully behind him. He says she bolted it, and I believe him. . . . She returned to her bedroom. . . . She undressed. . . . She was sitting on her bed, and had already taken off one of her stockings when . . . no, Monsieur Spencer, it wasn't Dandurand. . . . He didn't go back upstairs or open the front door or . . .

"And yet, four days later, he didn't hesitate, almost in my presence, to bring suspicion on himself by going back into that room. . . . What for?

"Remember that the old woman's papers—receipts, property deeds, all the documents she kept in the desk in her sitting room, in fact—none of any value to her murderer, since he couldn't make use of them without giving himself away—have vanished. . . .

"The bills, on the other hand, which in theory at least are untraceable, were left in their hiding place. Even if they were removed for a short while, they were subsequently put back. . . . How do you like these *cèpes à la bordelaise*?"

"Your mind must be on other things, if I may say so, Chief Superintendent, or you would have noticed that I have already had three helpings, and if I hadn't been promised *coq au vin* to follow . . . As for the Beaujolais, all I can say is that if you find me rather a dull companion this afternoon, you'll know why."

"Wait till you've tasted the *coq au vin*! . . . The proprietress worked twenty years as cook for a cabinet minister. He came to a dubious end, but he did appreciate good cooking. . . . Would you believe that Juliette was quite a beauty in her day? There's a photograph of her in the apartment. I wonder if, by any chance, her husband was a jealous man. . . ."

Having said this, he became once again lost in thought, from which he did not emerge until the proprietress came to the table to inquire whether the *coq au vin* had been to his liking. Every now and then, Maigret would glance toward the door.

"Are you expecting someone?"

"I'm expecting a visit from a gentleman who is not one

of my favorite characters. Apparently he's done nothing but hang around the Quai des Orfèvres for the past two days. I've arranged for him to meet me here."

A few minutes later, a taxi drew up outside. Maître Leloup, fat and self-important, paid the driver and came into the bistro.

"I've brought those papers I mentioned, as promised," he announced, putting down his leather brief case on an unoccupied table.

"As you will see presently, my valued client, Monsieur Monfils, was not exaggerating when he claimed . . ."

The lawyer had probably had no lunch, but the Chief Superintendent did not invite him to share their meal, nor did he suggest that he should take off his coat.

"I'll look into all that later."

"How is the case progressing?"

"Slowly, Maître Leloup . . . slowly."

"May I venture to draw your attention to one point which may have escaped your notice. Please don't imagine for one moment that I'm criticizing the methods for which you are justly famous. . . . But I, for my part, have not been idle. I made it my business to send someone to Fontenay, a thoroughly reliable man, to interview various elderly persons who had known Madame Boynet as a girl, when she was still Juliette Cazenove . . ."

Maigret, unimpressed, went on eating. He seemed to take no interest in what was being said. The American, watching, could not make him out.

"I learned one or two things which I think will surprise you. . . ."

At this, almost under his breath, the Chief Superintendent murmured:

"I very much doubt it. . . ."

"Juliette Cazenove had the reputation of being a rather flighty girl, at least in her conduct with men. . . ."

"And she is reputed to have been the mistress of

Charles Dandurand, is that it?"

"Who told you?"

"Nobody told me, but I thought it probable. . . . Dandurand was about ten years older than she was. . . . No doubt, even as long ago as that, he had developed a taste for unripe fruit."

"It created quite a scandal at the time. . . ."

"Not such a scandal, apparently, as to prevent Juliette from marrying her building contractor and moving with him to Paris. . . . None of this is news to me, Maître Leloup."

"What do you make of it?"

"I don't make anything of it. . . . It's too soon to jump. . . Ah, there's the telephone. I bet you it's for me. . . ."

Wearing an eager expression, he hurried to the phone. The call must have been for him, because he was away for some minutes. He came back looking relieved.

"Let's have some more of your *coq au vin, patron.*"

He realized suddenly that up to now he had barely touched his food. He was feeling quite peckish. He drank a whole glass of Beaujolais, and wiped his mouth on the back of his hand. His eyes sparkled.

"They've found Gérard!" he said at last, with a sigh. "Poor kid . . . !"

"Why do you say 'poor kid'?"

"Because he's been behaving like the idiot he is. . . . Another bottle, Désiré. . . . Would you believe it, he tried to get to the Belgian frontier by train, just as I said he would. When he got there, he found that the carriages were being searched more thoroughly than usual. He lost his head and jumped out of the train on the wrong side. He started running across the fields, stumbling through puddles and mud, with the police force close at his heels. He made a dash for the first farm he came to. . . . Can you guess where they found him when they caught up with him at last, after searching for an hour? . . . In the lavatory. . . .He resisted so violently that they practically had to knock him out. They're bringing him back to Paris. His train is due in at three-fifty."

"Has he confessed?" asked Maître Leloup.

Disingenuously, Maigret retorted:

"Confessed to what . . . ? Good God! I almost forgot the most important thing. I'd be obliged to you, Maître, if you would send a telegram to your client on my behalf. . . . In view of the good relations between him and his aunt Boynet, I've been wondering whether she ever put anything in his safe-keeping which she would have found embarrassing to keep in her apartment. . . . Don't ask me what! I've no idea! Maybe she used to send him presents . . . . I simply can't wait to hear!"

At last they were rid of the pestilential lawyer. They could savor Mélanie's coffee and Désiré's old Armagnac in peace. Désiré had come originally from the Gers region, and he had kept in touch with his old friends, many of whom owned vineyards. By now, they had the clean, plainly furnished little restaurant, with its steamy windows, all to themselves. The table had been wiped, and was now covered with the documents furnished by the lawyer. They were all letters, handwritten on the black-edged paper used by Juliette Boynet after she became a widow.

"My dear cousins,

"Thank you for your good wishes, which I heartily reciprocate. It is a sad state of affairs when an old woman like me finds herself surrounded by ungrateful people. When I think of all I have done for my sister's children, and how . . ."

As Maigret finished reading each of the letters, he handed it to his companion, who glanced through it in his turn. They were all alike, all dated the second or third of

January, since each was in reply to Monfils's New Year greetings.

"They can afford to be patient, believing as they do that they will one day inherit all I have. . . ."

And elsewhere:

"Gérard is a good-for-nothing who never comes near me except to ask for money. . . . As if it grew on trees . . . !"

Berthe fared no better.

"It's a great relief to have her off my hands. There was always the risk that she might be put into a condition, and think of the talk that would have caused among the neighbors. . . ."

"A condition?" echoed Mr. Oats, puzzled.

"An interesting condition. . . . It's a delicate way of saying that she feared that her niece might become pregnant. . . ."

They felt blissfully warm, with the flavor of the Armagnac on their palates and its aroma in their nostrils.

"It's a terrible affliction to be alone and helpless, and to realize that all anyone cares about is one's money. . . . I am haunted by the dread that, sooner or later, some misfortune may befall me. . . .

"You are fortunate to be living in your quiet little town, free from all the anxieties which are ruinous to one's health. Cécile makes a show of being devoted to me, but she's always ready to take her brother's part against me.

"And there is another person who is deeply indebted to me, but whom I cannot wholly trust. . . ."

Maigret pointed out this passage to his companion.

"There was no one whom she wholly trusted," he murmured.

"With good reason, surely?"

"Read the rest of it!"

"Luckily for me, I am not such a fool as they think, and I have taken certain precautions. . . . If anything happens to me, I can promise you they won't profit by it."

" *'They,'* " sighed Maigret. "As far as she was concerned, they were all tarred with the same brush, everyone who came near her, all those whom she suspected of envying her for her wealth, including Monsieur Dandurand. . . . Are you beginning to see . . . ?"

"To see what?"

Maigret smiled.

"I don't blame you. . . . I'm beginning to talk in innuendo, just as she did. . . . To see what, indeed? . . . I should have said 'feel' rather than 'see.' I'm afraid you must be feeling let down if, as you mentioned this morning, you were hoping to learn something from my method of work. . . . I've taken you sloshing through puddles, looking up old records in a dreary town hall, and I've fed you on *coq au vin*. . . . How can I explain myself to you? *I feel things*. . . . Dandurand, recently released from prison, comes to Paris and goes into furnished lodgings. . . . He seeks out Juliette, who is not yet a widow. . . . What kind of a man was her husband? We have nothing to go on but old photographs. A man of forty-five, tall, thickset, nondescript. Juliette and Dandurand resume their former relationship. No doubt they meet in Dandurand's rooms on Rue Delambre. The husband dies, and, as soon as he decently can, Dandurand moves into the same house as his mistress, though their relationship remains a well-kept secret."

"I can't see why they should have wanted to keep it secret," demurred the American.

There was a long silence. Maigret sat gazing at his glass. At length he sighed, and drank a mouthful of Armagnac.

Then he said abruptly:

"We shall see! . . . Désiré! . . . The check, if you please. If I get no work done this afternoon, I shall have you and your wife to thank for it.

"What was that bastard doing in Juliette's bedroom? For God's sake, Monsieur Spencer, can't you help me? Just think, if we could find the right answer to that question . . ."

Spencer Oats, like a model secretary, began gathering up the black-edged letters, which were spread out on the table.

"Taking precautions?" he ventured.

"Precautions?"

Maigret frowned.

Now he came to think of it, had not the old woman, in one of the letters, mentioned taking certain precautions to safeguard herself against those who were envious of her wealth? She had been mistrustful of everyone, including her former lover.

"How did you like the food, Monsieur Maigret?" asked the forthright Mélanie, who treated all her customers, some of whom were celebrities, with motherly familiarity. "You remember that recipe I wrote out for Madame Maigret? Has she tried it yet?"

The Chief Superintendent was not listening. After putting his change in his trouser pocket he did not even take out his hand, but sat staring at the proprietress's apron in a state of suspended animation.

At long last, he said:

"What I couldn't make out was why Cécile was killed. . . . Do you see, Monsieur Spencer? Everything else could be explained. . . . It was easy. . . . But Cécile is dead, and . . . Sorry, Mélanie. Thanks for the lunch. We thoroughly enjoyed it. Even if my friend remembers nothing else, I'm sure it will provide him with a topic of conversation when he goes back to Philadelphia."

He was in a highly nervous state. As they walked along the street he said not a word, and when at last they reached the corner of Avenue d'Orléans, he waved down a taxi.

"Quai des Orfèvres, and hurry!"

They were almost halfway there when he changed his mind.

"Take us to the Gare du Nord first . . . Inter-City arrivals. . . . It's later than I thought. . . ."

Was it perhaps due to the *coq au vin*, the Beaujolais, Mélanie's homemade coffee-cream cake, and Désiré's Armagnac? At any rate, whatever the reason, Spencer Oats was looking at his preoccupied companion with a good deal of affection. In the past few hours, it seemed to him, he had been witnessing a series of metamorphoses. The Chief Superintendent, huddled in his overcoat, his bowler hat on the back of his head and his pipe clenched between his teeth, had been actually living the lives of all the characters, the perverted, the miserly, the pitiful, in the drama that it was his responsibility to resolve.

"It may be that, at this very moment, his wife is in labor . . ."

His cheeks were flushed, as if he himself were the anxious husband. Maigret was right there on the train, flanked by two guards, in Gérard's place. He was beside Berthe, watching over Gérard's wife.

He was in the house in Bourg-la-Reine, resting his feet on old Juliette's tapestry stool, or on the floor below, in the apartment from which Monsieur Charles could hear everything that went on overhead.

Every now and then, when they were held up at a busy crossroads by the white baton of a traffic policeman in a cape, Maigret would catch sight of the moonlike face of an electric clock and, haunted by a sense of time lost, would rise half out of his seat, as if to lighten the driver's load and enable him to cover the ground more quickly.

They reached the Gare du Nord just in the nick of time. In fact, they very nearly didn't make it. A crowd of spectators. A policeman was shouting:

"Move along there!"

Then they caught sight of a thin young man in handcuffs, pushed jerkily forward by two policemen, like a horse between the shafts. His trousers were spattered with mud, his raincoat torn. And this feverish, petulant youth, Gérard, no doubt seemed to the bystanders the very incarnation of the thwarted criminal!

His lips trembled when he saw the Chief Superintendent.

"You think you're very clever, I'm sure. . . ."

Maigret showed his badge to the two policemen and ushered them into the waiting taxi.

They got in with alacrity. They were in a lather. They had been on edge throughout the train journey for fear that their charge might take it into his head to jump out onto the line.

"I don't suppose anyone has bothered to inquire after my wife!"

And big tears trickled from between his swollen eyelids which he was unable to wipe away because of the handcuffs.

Three

"Where have you come from?"

"Feignes, Chief Superintendent."

"You could catch the five-seven train back . . . unless you'd prefer to spend the night in Paris? Let's have your expense sheets, boys."

Maigret stopped the taxi on the corner of Rue La Fayette. It was such a squally day that people were having difficulty in holding their umbrellas upright. At the sight of a taxi full of police, the passers-by stopped and stared. The Chief Superintendent spread the expense sheets on his knee and signed them. The two policemen got out and disappeared into a bar. Maigret slid back the glass panel and, in an undertone, murmured something to the driver; then, as soon as the taxi was in motion again, he took a small key from his pocket and relieved Gérard Pardon of his handcuffs.

"I expect you to behave yourself, if you don't mind. . . . A few dozen blameless citizens like you, and we would have to treble the personnel of the Police Judiciaire."

Gérard gave a start. He had been gazing out at the streets of Paris as if he had not set eyes on them for years. Now, he turned his permanently mistrustful gaze upon the Chief Superintendent.

"What makes you say 'blameless'?"

Maigret had difficulty in suppressing a smile.

"You're surely not telling me that you are guilty?"

"If you believed I was innocent, why did you have me arrested?"

"If you really are innocent, why did you run away? Why did you bolt like a frightened horse at the sight of a couple of policemen? And why did you go to ground in a little cubbyhole which could hardly have been conducive to comfort?"

Spencer Oats, leaning back in his seat, was blissfully digesting his lunch. He was smiling faintly, as people do when, after a good dinner, they are sitting in a theater, indulgently watching the twists and turns of an exciting play. The light inside the taxi was greenish, as though filtered through the frosted glass panes of a lantern.

Through the cab windows everything looked distorted, the people, the buildings, and the umbrellas colliding at strange angles. Sometimes, when the traffic was held up, they could see a bus, with all its passengers in frozen attitudes like waxworks.

"Look, my boy. I know who killed your aunt."

"Not really!"

"I know who killed your aunt, and I will prove it to you shortly."

"It's impossible . . ." protested Gérard stubbornly, shaking his head. "No one could possibly know . . ."

"Except you, do you mean? *And yet I'm as sure as I am of anything that you slept through it all!*"

This really did shake Cécile's brother. He looked at Maigret in horrified amazement, as if he could not believe his ears.

"There! You see . . ."

"But . . . Where are we going?"

Everything was shrouded in a Scotch mist, and Pardon had only just realized that they were near Place de la Bastille. Because of the one-way system, the driver was approaching Place des Vosges by way of Rue Saint-Antoine.

"Now, just you listen to me. There is a reward of twenty thousand francs for information leading to the apprehension of the killer. For reasons which don't concern you, the Police Judiciaire want no part of that money."

"But . . . you must know that I . . ."

"Just you keep your mouth shut! To the best of my knowledge, your wife is still at home, and your sister Berthe is with her.

"As you appear to have some objection to the Maternity Ward, here is something on account, which you can set against the twenty thousand francs you will be receiving shortly. Go on up! Be as quick as you can. We'll wait for you in the cab. What clinic did you have in mind when you asked Cécile for the money?"

"Saint Joseph's. . . ."

"Very well, Berthe can take your wife there now, and you can join them later on!"

The American looked from one to the other in some bewilderment.

"Don't do anything foolish, now!"

The taxi had stopped, but Gérard, dazed and perhaps still a little mistrustful, hesitated.

"Be off with you, you silly fool!"

For the next ten minutes, Maigret smoked his pipe in silence; and when, presently, Pardon reappeared, wiping his eyes, he merely exchanged glances with Spencer Oats.

"Quai des Orfèvres, driver. . . . By the way, Gérard, when did you last have anything to eat?"

"*They* gave me a sandwich on the train. . . . But really, I'm not hungry. I *am* thirsty, though. The . . . I . . ."

He was so overcome that he could hardly speak.

They stopped once again outside a bar. Maigret was thankful for the chance to order a glass of beer to help him digest the *coq au vin*, not to mention the coffee-cream cake.

Ten minutes later, he was stuffing his stove with all the fuel it could take. After he had lit it and switched on the green-shaded table lamp on his desk, he said to Gérard:

"Sit down. . . . Take off your raincoat, it's soaking. . . . Come nearer the fire. Your trousers will soon be dry. You must have been out of your mind to get yourself into such a state!"

It was not yet quite dark. Through the window could be seen strings of faintly glimmering lights all along the banks of the Seine. It was the busiest time of the day at police headquarters. Doors could be heard opening and shutting, footsteps hurried to and fro in the corridor, telephones rang, typewriters chattered.

"Torrence! That list you made out for me of all visitors to this building on the morning of the seventh of October, bring it here, will you. . . ."

At long last, Maigret sat down, picked up the biggest of the many pipes ranged on his desk, and began:

"What did you have to drink that night, at your aunt's apartment? . . . Wait . . . let me help you. . . . You were at the end of your tether, weren't you? You knew that your child was due any moment, and you hadn't so much as a stitch of clothing for it. You were in the habit of going to your sister Cécile for money. . . . Come now! You needn't look so sheepish. . . . Unfortunately, Cécile hadn't much to give, only what she could save out of the housekeeping, and her allowance was far from generous. As a rule, you waited for your sister outside in the street. But that night you went upstairs and let yourself into the apartment. You hid in Cécile's bedroom while she was elsewhere attending to Madame Boynet. . . . Am I right so far?"

"Quite right. . . ."

"When your aunt was settled at the dining-room table and ready for her dinner, Cécile went into the kitchen. You opened the bedroom door and told her that you had to have some money *at all costs*."

"I told her I was at the end of my tether, and rather than see my wife . . ."

"Right. . . . Not only did you play on Cécile's sympathy, you went further, *you frightened her. . . . It was a sort of emotional blackmail.*"

"I had made up my mind to kill myself."

"After having killed your wife! . . . Idiot!"

"I swear to you, Chief Superintendent, I would have done it. . . . For three whole days before that, I . . ."

"Shut up. . . . Your sister couldn't discuss the matter with you then, in case the old woman should overhear. She served the meal as usual. . . . She ate with her aunt. . . . No doubt she asked the old woman for the money, and was refused? By the time Madame Boynet was safely in bed—I presume she did go to bed?—it was too late for you to leave the house, as by that time the street door was locked. You would have had to ask the concierge to let you out, and she might have reported it to her employer. Presumably Cécile brought food to you in the bedroom? What did you have to eat?"

"Bread and cheese."

"Did you have anything to drink?"

"A glass of wine, to start with . . ."

"Anything else?"

"Cécile always had a cup of herb tea at night, because she had a delicate stomach. There was a full cup there ready for her. She suggested that I should drink it. I had been crying. I was feeling very low, and I thought I was going to be sick . . ."

"And Cécile gave up her bed to you?"

"Yes. . . . We talked a little while longer about Hélène. . . . Then, I can't think why, I fell asleep. . . ."

Maigret looked at the American as if to say: I told you so.

"You fell asleep because you drank the herb tea intended for your sister, to which your aunt, as always when she was expecting a visit from Monsieur Charles, had added a massive dose of bromide. . . . Everything that followed occurred as a result of this seemingly trivial mischance. If Cécile had drunk the herb tea as intended, your aunt would almost certainly still be alive, in which case your sister . . ."

Maigret got up and went to the window. He stood there with his back to the room and murmured, as if to himself:

"Cécile, having given up her bed to you, sits in an armchair. . . . She can't get to sleep, and for a very good reason. . . . Old Madame Boynet, as the appointed time approaches, gets up, puts on her dressing gown and stockings and, confident that there is no one to hear her, goes to the door to wait for Monsieur Charles. It was all because you were feeling sick, and therefore drank the herb tea intended for Cécile, that the two schemers . . ."

"What do you mean by that?" exclaimed the young man, turning pale.

"Isn't that what they were? Come now, let me finish. . . . It's getting very hot in here. . . ."

He went across and opened a door leading to another office.

"As I was saying, the two schemers are in the sitting room, which is lit only by a single table lamp. Cécile, hearing noises, creeps into the passage or the dining room and listens unseen. They talk in low voices of their unsavory business affairs . . . about the house in Béziers . . . and the one on Rue d'Antin. . . . I can just imagine poor Cécile's face when, at long last, it dawned on her what sort of places they were. Monsieur Charles hands over the fifty thousand francs to his former mistress. She relocks the bureau, but retains the money in her hand. She sees the former lawyer to the door, and bolts it behind him. Breathing a sigh of satisfaction, she returns to her bedroom. A good night's work . . . a substantial addition to her savings. She raises the lid of the tapestry stool which she uses as a strongbox, and Cécile, her eye glued to the keyhole, sees the thick bundles of thousand-franc bills. As for you, you are still sound asleep. . . . *Were you awakened by any untoward sounds?* Think carefully now."

"No . . . it was my sister who . . ."

"Hold on. . . . Your aunt is undressing. . . . She has already taken off one stocking when Cécile, driven frantic by your threats of suicide . . ."

"I couldn't have foreseen.. . ." wailed Gérard.

"That's what they always say afterward. . . . But be that as it may, your sister bursts into the room, much to the alarm of the old woman. The sight of all that money, a fortune no less, gives Cécile courage. She repeats her request for money. She is not pleading now, she is almost threatening. . . . *What neither of the two women suspects is that, in the apartment below, Monsieur Charles is listening, in astonishment and alarm, to every word they say*. I can guess your aunt's reaction. No doubt she tongue-lashed her niece, whom she considered to be so much in her debt, and reminded her yet again of all she had done for her and her family. Possibly she may even have threatened to call for help?"

"It wasn't quite like that . . ." said the young man slowly.

"In that case, you tell me!"

"I don't know exactly what time it was . . . I heard someone calling my name over and over again. . . . Waking up was a struggle, and I couldn't make out what was going on. I felt dazed, as if I'd had too much to drink. Cécile was sitting on the edge of the bed. . . .

" *'Gérard!'* she shouted, *'Gérard! What's wrong with you? You've got to listen to me!'*

"She was very composed, more so than usual. . . . I thought she must be ill, she was so pale and she had such dark rings under her eyes. . . . She spoke softly, but distinctly.

" *'Gérard . . . Aunt Juliette is dead. . . . I've just killed her.'*

"And then she sat quite still for ages, just staring at the floor.

"I got out of bed, intending to go and see for myself.

" *'Don't move. . . . You mustn't on any account!'* "

"She didn't want your fingerprints to be found there," murmured Maigret.

He was thinking of Cécile, impassive, waiting for him for hours on end in the "aquarium."

"That's what she told me. . . . She described it all to me. Aunt Juliette was sitting on the edge of the bed. She must have heard something, because she felt under her pillow for the revolver she always kept there at night. She was scared stiff of burglars.

" *'Oh, it's you!'* she said, on seeing Cécile. *'Why aren't you asleep? I suppose you've been spying on me. . . .'*

" *'Listen, Aunt . . . Earlier tonight, I asked you for a little money for Gérard, or rather for his wife, who is expecting a baby.'*

" *'Go back to bed!'*

" *'You're a rich woman. . . . I know that now. . . . You've got to listen to me. . . . Gérard will kill himself if . . .'*

" *'Is that good-for-nothing brother of yours here?'*

"My aunt, still holding the revolver, tried to stand up. Cécile was so scared, she went up to her and seized her by the arm. . . .

" *'You've got to give me some money!'*

"Aunt Juliette fell back on the bed. She struggled to reach the revolver, which had slipped out of her hand. And it was then that my sister seized her by the throat."

"In cold blood!" Maigret's voice rang out with unwonted resonance.

Yes, he had been wrong. There had been no commotion. Cécile had not lost her head. If ever there was a sheep in human form, it had been Cécile. For years and years she had been submissive without even realizing it, meekness came to her so naturally. It had not taken much, just the sight of that pile of bills, to make her realize the extent to which her aunt had duped and exploited her.

"Go on, my boy."

"For a long time, we sat in silence. . . . At one point Cécile left me, to make sure that Aunt Juliette was really dead.

"When at last she did speak, it was to say:

" 'The police will have to be told. . . .' "

In Maigret's office, too, there was a long silence. The gray dusk was pierced only by the green-shaded desk light, which revealed the features of the two men in sharp relief. The only sound was the sputter of a pipe.

Maigret could picture the brother and sister together in the apartment, in that great house abutting on the Route Nationale, overwhelmed and utterly stunned by what had happened. And in the apartment below, Monsieur Charles, panic-stricken, able to hear everything, even the faintest whisper.

"If I were to go up now . . ."

And Cécile, looking thoughtfully at her brother. The police were never going to believe that he had taken no part in the murder. Both were sick at heart, and as exhausted as if they had been running for hours.

Should she try and get him out of the house? But that would mean asking the concierge to release the catch, and she would be bound to look out through the spyhole to see who it was leaving the house at this late hour. The brother and sister started as all the clocks in the apartment chimed the hour.

"Listen, Gérard . . . I'll go and see Chief Superintendent Maigret first thing in the morning. . . . I'll tell him everything. . . . And, while the concierge is out in the yard collecting the garbage cans, you can safely slip out of here and go home."

A strange vigil, indeed! They were utterly cut off from the rest of the world. Their plight conjured up a picture of refugees squatting on the ground, surrounded by bundles, in station waiting rooms or on board ship.

"Which one of you," inquired Maigret, relighting his pipe, "thought of the idea of opening the desk and examining the papers?"

"It was Cécile. . . . But that was much later. She had just made coffee for the two of us. I was still pretty dazed. . . . We were sitting in the kitchen, and she suddenly whispered:

" *'Supposing that man should come back . . .'*

"And she went on:

" *'Well, I did tell the Chief Superintendent that someone had been coming up to the apartment at night. . . . But he wouldn't believe me. . . . And now . . .'* "

Maigret stared at the unadorned rectangle of the window and bit on the stem of his pipe.

" *'Heaven knows what he may do while we're out. . . .'* "

Whereupon Cécile had calmly suggested removing the papers from the desk. It had never crossed her mind to take the money and run, or even to give some of it to her brother in his dire need.

"Did you look through the papers yourself?" asked the Chief Superintendent.

"Yes."

At this point, Maigret got up and went across to the door of the little side office, which he had already pushed open a few minutes before.

"I think you had better join us in here, Monsieur Dandurand. . . . What we are about to discuss chiefly concerns you."

For it was none other than Monsieur Charles installed in the adjoining office under the watchful eye of an inspector. He cut rather a sorry figure, stripped of his collar and tie and even his shoelaces. He had not shaved for two days. His hands hung down in front of him, joined at the wrists by handcuffs.

"I'm afraid I can't offer you a chair. I'm sorry, you must be very tired."

Gérard sprang to his feet, suspecting a trap.

"What on earth . . . ?"

"Calm down, Pardon. . . . Carry on with what you were saying. . . . I want Monsieur Dandurand to hear your story. . . . You had reached the point where you and your sister were together in the sitting room, looking through the papers in your aunt's desk. Mostly, I imagine, they related to money matters, bills, receipts, accounts, and that sort of thing."

"There were some letters as well."

As he said this, Gérard stole a glance at the former lawyer, as if fearful, in spite of the handcuffs, that he might assault him.

"Love letters, were they not?"

At this, the former lawyer intervened:

"One moment! May I ask if this is by way of being a confrontation?"

"You might call it that, Monsieur Dandurand."

"In that case, I should be obliged if you would permit me to call my lawyer. . . . Indeed, I insist. It is my right under the law . . ."

"What is your lawyer's name?"

"Maître Planchard."

"Torrence! Torrence!" shouted Maigret. "Call Maître Planchard, will you? One moment, though. . . . At this hour I should think he must be in court."

"He's in Court Eleven," interposed Monsieur Charles.

"Go across to Court Eleven, and bring him here. If his case is still in progress, tell him to ask for an adjournment . . . at my request."

For the next half hour or so, complete silence reigned in Maigret's office, during which time the slightest movement was as audible as the plop of a pebble in a pond.

"Take a seat, Maître Planchard. . . . I had better tell you frankly at the outset that it is my present intention to apply to the Examining Magistrate for a warrant for the arrest of your client on a charge of premeditated murder. Pay attention, Pardon. . . . Just now you referred to certain love letters. If I am not mistaken, these letters date back some fifteen years."

"I don't know. . . . None of them was dated."

The lawyer smiled triumphantly and seemed on the point of adopting a tone of forensic belligerency. But Maigret forestalled him by addressing himself to Spencer Oats:

"You recall our visit to the ugly little town hall in Bourg-la-Reine?"

Then, turning to Gérard:

"What was in those letters? No, wait. . . . We'd better get one important point clear first. . . . Am I right in thinking that your sister took the letters so seriously that she made up her mind to hand them over to me when she came here, to police headquarters, to give herself up? She put them in her bag, did she not, along with all the other papers from the desk?"

"Yes."

"In that case," interposed the lawyer, turning to Maigret, "I'd be obliged if you would produce these documents."

"Let us take our time, Maître."

At this, Maigret noted, an ambiguous smile played about Monsieur Charles's lips.

"You're not out of the wood yet, Dandurand! . . . Oh! I'm well aware that those all-too-compromising letters fell into your hands, and that you destroyed them. . . . *But don't forget that, while I was engaged on the telephone in your apartment, you seized the opportunity to go upstairs and into*

Madame Boynet's bedroom. . . . Now then, Gérard, let's have the rest of your story. First of all, tell us how the writer of the letters addressed the recipient."

"They all began: 'My darling . . .' "

It seemed, all of a sudden, as if Maigret was enjoying himself.

"Sorry to interrupt you again, but I feel I owe an explanation to my American colleague . . . I shouldn't like him to get any wrong ideas about how love affairs are conducted in France, and I would therefore wish to point out that, when those letters were written, Madame Boynet was fifteen years younger. Even though she was no longer in the first flush of youth, she was, nevertheless, a very different person from the dreadful old fright hobbling on a cane that she was to become in her later years. . . . How many letters were there, Gérard?"

"About thirty. . . . Most of them were just notes . . . *'Tomorrow, at three . . . usual place . . . love and kisses . . . Yours . . .'* "

"Any signature?"

"They were all signed 'C.' "

Monsieur Charles, who had not been invited to sit down, never took his eyes off the young man. His face was ashen, but he was still very much in command of himself.

"A mere initial doesn't prove anything," objected Maître Planchard. "If these letters are produced in evidence, I shall enlist the services of a handwriting expert."

"They will not be produced in evidence. . . . *At least, not those letters*. . . . Go on, Gérard. Some of the letters were longer, were they not?"

"There were four or five that were. . . ."

"Tell us about them."

"In one of them, I remember he wrote: *'Be brave! Remember, your deliverance is at hand, and in a few weeks' time, we shall have peace at last.'* "

Maître Planchard sniggered:

"Are you suggesting that she was pregnant?"

"No, sir! I am suggesting that here was a woman with two men in her power, her husband and her lover. This letter was written by her lover."

"Was her husband ill, is that what you are saying?"

"That's what we shall have to find out. Go on, my boy."

And Gérard, uncomfortably aware that he was the focus of all eyes, stammered:

"In another letter he wrote: *'You see, he doesn't suspect a thing. . . . Be patient! I think it would be wiser for us not to meet for the time being. . . . On the present dose, there will be a delay of at least a fortnight. It would be too risky to attempt to hasten the outcome.'* "

"I don't understand!" exclaimed the lawyer, with a little cough.

"That's just too bad, Maître . . ."

"And besides, I'm still waiting for you to produce the documents under discussion. Permit me to say that I consider it most unwise of you to proceed on the basis . . ."

Whereupon Maigret, very bland and suave, broke in:

"If you insist, I am prepared to order the exhumation of the late Joseph Boynet and institute tests on what remains of him after fifteen years. . . . You are no doubt aware, Maître, that most poisons, especially poisons such as arsenic, which can be administered in very small quantities, leave traces which remain in the body for a very long time after . . ."

He was interrupted by Torrence, with the list he had asked for of everyone who had visited police headquarters on the morning of Cécile's murder.

Four

"You must be tired of standing, Dandurand. . . . Torrence! Bring in another chair. Monsieur Charles is looking a bit shaky."

"You are mistaken, Chief Superintendent. . . . I'm still waiting for you to produce so much as a shred of evidence . . ."

"Give me a chance! In view of the fact that your legal adviser, Maître Planchard, never met old Juliette, I feel it only right that I should give him a brief description of the lady. . . . Don't you agree, Maître Planchard?"

The lawyer assented with a slight nod, and lit a cigarette.

"Juliette Cazenove, as she then was, growing up in the township of Fontenay-le-Comte, became Dandurand's mistress at a very early age. . . . It created quite a scandal locally. Monsieur Dandurand, at that time, did not yet have any convictions for the corruption of minors. . . . He was very much younger in those days, and not unattractive, I assume. All the same, when the opportunity of making a good match presented itself in the person of Joseph Boynet, Juliette, the child of impoverished parents, didn't hesitate. She even went so far as to sacrifice her sister by appropriating her dowry to add to her own. . . .

"What sort of life did she envisage for herself in Paris as the wife of a prosperous building contractor? Who can tell?

"She went to live in Bourg-la-Reine. . . . A jealous husband . . . a dull existence . . . certainly not luxurious. . . .

"Years passed. . . . Back in Fontenay her former lover, Monsieur Dandurand, grew older but did not outgrow his taste for young girls, which later developed into a passion for very young girls. . . .

"But we won't go into that, if you don't mind. A two-year prison sentence. . . . Nothing much, really. . . .

"And then, one fine day, he turns up in Paris, in furnished rooms on Rue Delambre, debarred forever not only from his own profession but from respectable society as a whole. . . .

"Where did they meet again? It doesn't matter. Suffice it to say that they became lovers once more. And before long the husband was getting in their way. . . .

"In Juliette's way, especially. I'm quite sure of that. It may even have been her idea to get rid of the husband who stood in the way of her freedom. . . .

"That she sought and obtained the advice of her lover we know from his letters. . . ."

"Letters which I challenge you to produce!" interrupted the lawyer, making a show of referring to his papers.

"Letters which I shall not produce, because, on their account, your client was driven to commit a second murder, and that's a fact."

"In that case . . ."

A broad sweep of the arm. The lawyer had perhaps forgotten that he was not in a courtroom, wearing his black gown with its billowing sleeves.

"Patience, my dear Maître. . . . The husband dies at last. . . . The husband is dead. . . . He was given to overeating, heavy drinking, and overwork. . . . His doctor is easily persuaded that the cause of death is a heart attack. And it was at this point . . ."

He paused, turning first to Monsieur Charles, then to Spencer Oats, his eyes alight with mischief:

"And it was at this point that our friend Juliette turned

overnight into the crazy old woman of her later years! Possibly she was still attracted to the man who had been her accomplice, but she was also afraid of him. . . . She became deeply suspicious of everything, because she now knew how easy it was to take a life. She became a miser. Monsieur Charles went to live in her house, occupying the apartment just below hers; but she had become jealous of her reputation, and would only meet him outside. . . . Then, out of the blue, two nieces and a nephew fell into her lap. . . . Later, on account of her infirmities, she ceased to be able to go out, and in order to confer in safety with her accomplice at night she took the precaution of drugging Cécile with bromide. . . . If Cécile had not had a weak stomach . . . if she had not been in the habit of drinking herb tea every night, God knows . . .

"Madame Boynet had kept those old letters safely locked up in her desk in the sitting room. . . . Dandurand had put her in the way of a number of highly profitable, even though unsavory, investments. . . . She, who had once been a passionate lover, was now old, miserly, and helpless. . . . As illicit relationships go, this was a particularly odious one. The nephew and one of the nieces had escaped, and good riddance to them! Only poor Cécile, endowed with the temperament of a slave or a saint, stuck it out."

"Permit me to ask you a question, Chief Superintendent," put in the lawyer. "What are your grounds for . . . ?"

"I'll tell you later, Maître. In the meantime, I would appreciate your attention for a little while longer. . . . Love had turned to avarice. One passion had been superseded by another, because, as every blacksmith knows, it takes a nail to knock out a nail. It took only the merest mischance, the trivial accident whereby Gérard drank the herb tea intended for Cécile, for the situation to explode into tragedy. . . .

"Dandurand, downstairs in his apartment, hears every word. He knows that up there now there are two people who have just learned the whole truth. He knows that Cécile has made up her mind to tell me everything, to hand over the letters to me. . . .

"Dare he take the risk of going up to the fifth floor, right then, in the middle of the night, to forestall . . . ?

"You must have had a rough night of it, Dandurand."

Dandurand did not flinch. On the contrary, he responded with his usual bleak, fleeting smile.

"Early next morning, while the concierge is out in the yard with her garbage cans, the brother and sister creep downstairs. Dandurand, his door open a crack, sees them go by. If only Cécile were by herself! But he couldn't tackle two people at once. . . .

"Out in the street, the brother and sister go their separate ways. Dandurand follows Cécile in the fog, hoping for a chance at least to snatch her bag and its incriminating contents.

"The streetcar is not the right place . . . Between Pont Saint-Michel and police headquarters, no opportunity arises. . . .

"She is inside the building. . . . She is going up the stairs. . . . Can anything save Monsieur Charles now?

"But there is one thing on his side: time. . . . It is not yet eight o'clock. . . . I am still at home. . . . And that morning, as it so happens, I decide, for no particular reason, except perhaps to savor Paris in the fog, to walk to work. Meanwhile, Cécile is waiting for me in the room we call the 'aquarium.' Dandurand meanwhile is lurking nearby."

"Forgive me, Chief Superintendent, but I feel obliged to repeat my question: Have you any proof? Have you any witnesses?"

"I have here in front of me, Maître Planchard, a list of everyone who entered this building on the morning in question, and I see that there are at least three names . . . You, who are, in a sense, one of us, must surely understand . . . It would have been much too risky for Dandurand to go up and speak to Cécile himself. Knowing all there was to know, nothing on earth would have persuaded her to go anywhere with him. . . .

"But as luck would have it, who should turn up just then at police headquarters but a shady youth, a member of that very fraternity of which Monsieur Charles had established himself as a leading light . . .

"Dandurand accosts him eagerly:

" *'Hi there! There's a wench up there waiting to see the Chief Superintendent, and she's got to be stopped. . . . It's absolutely essential that I should have a word with her. . . . She doesn't know you. . . .'*

"Bear in mind that Dandurand knows his way about the corridors of this building and those of the Palais de Justice as well as we do.

" *'Think of some excuse to bring her to me . . . I'll be waiting beyond the glass door that . . . !'*

"And that, gentlemen, is the only way it could have been managed. Needless to say, the accomplice had no notion that a murder was about to be committed, or he would have been reluctant, I assume, to do as he was asked, and I'm quite sure he's regretted it since. . . . And so the drama unfolds:

" *'Do you wish to see Chief Superintendent Maigret?'*

"Cécile has just seen me go past. . . . She is waiting. . . . Unsuspectingly, she follows the spurious messenger. . . .

"He leads her through the glass door. . . .

"You'd be wise to admit that that's how it happened, Dandurand, *because it is the only way it could have happened!*

"At the sight of you, she is terrified. The broom closet is close at hand. You push her. She struggles. You try to grab her bag, but she clings to it. You strike her, and then . . ."

"All this is pure conjecture, Chief Superintendent."

The lawyer, who had been making copious notes, had lost none of his composure. After all, in such cases, it is not the lawyer's neck that is in jeopardy.

And then, directing an almost imperceptible wink at his transatlantic colleague, Maigret murmured:

"Would a letter meet the case?"

"A letter from the man who took Cécile to my client?"

"A letter from your client himself, my dear Maître."

Dandurand's expression was steely.

"Show it to me, then. I'm waiting."

"And I," sighed Maigret, "am waiting for it to be found."

"In other words, all this is . . ."

"Pure conjecture . . . yes, I'm afraid so. . . . All the same, Monsieur Charles did slip away from me and go into Juliette's bedroom. . . . And he must have had a reason for doing so. . . . I have instituted a thorough search of the room. . . . I don't know if you are familiar with the workings of an old woman's mind. Old women, as a class, tend to be deeply suspicious. Even though she did keep most of the letters in her desk, you can take it from me that . . ."

Monsieur Dandurand sniggered. They all stared at him.

At this point, if the truth were told, Maigret was very close to admitting defeat.

He had only one shred of hope to cling to. Had not Juliette Boynet said, in one of her letters to Monfils, that if any mishap should befall her . . . ?

The Chief Superintendent had staked his all on this. He still refused to believe that, during those few minutes alone in the bedroom, Dandurand had . . .

The very fact that he had gone into that room, lifted the lid of the tapestry stool and touched the bundles of bills, even at the risk of leaving fingerprints, and yet had not taken them, must surely mean that he had been looking for something else, which was even more important to him.

Was it conceivable that the old woman had been so foolish as to keep so crucial a document in the apartment, where he could find it?

And what if Maître Leloup had failed to telegraph to Monfils? What if Monfils had gone off fishing or shooting or whatever? What if he were anywhere but at home? If . . . ?

The telephone rang. Maigret quite literally leaped upon the instrument.

"Hello! . . . Yes. . . . Very well. . . . Keep trying."

As he replaced the receiver, try as he might to conceal the fact, his face told Spencer Oats more plainly than words that the search in the apartment at Bourg-la-Reine had yielded nothing.

"Permit me to point out, Chief Superintendent . . ."

"You can point out anything you wish. . . . As things are . . ."

"Your entire case rests upon a nonexistent letter, and, in these circumstances, as you know, my client has the right to . . ."

The telephone rang again.

"Hello! . . . Very well! . . . Three or four hours? . . . Yes, he's here. I'll tell him."

And turning to Gérard:

"You'd better go to your wife. I don't think it will be long now before you are a father."

"I repeat, Chief Superintendent, that . . ."

Maigret gave the lawyer a look, but said nothing. Then he turned to the American, winked, and went out with him into the corridor.

"It's beginning to look," he said, "as if this case, in which you have been so good as to take an interest, will end by making me look an awful fool, and you will go back to the United States with a very poor impression of my methods. . . . All the same, I'm certain, absolutely certain, d'you see, that . . ."

And then, abruptly and without preamble, Maigret interrupted himself:

"What do you say to a beer?"

He hustled his companion out. In passing, he looked broodingly into the "aquarium," where two or three people were waiting.

They walked along in the shadow of the Palais de Justice and went into the Brasserie Dauphine, which was quiet and warm, and redolent of draught beer.

"Two beers! . . . Bumpers!"

"What's a bumper?" asked the American.

"It's a special glass, reserved for regulars. . . . It holds a full liter. . . ."

Somewhat inflated, they retraced their steps.

"I could swear . . . Oh, well, never mind! If I have to start again from scratch, so be it."

Spencer Oats was in the state of embarrassment felt by a man who attempts to express condolences without resorting to outworn phrases.

"Do you understand? Psychologically speaking, I know I'm right. . . . It isn't possible that . . ."

"What if Dandurand got to the letter first?"

"Show me the lover that can match his mistress in cunning!" retorted the Chief Superintendent. "And old Juliette . . ."

They went up the dusty staircase, patterned with damp footprints. A man came up to them, self-important and very much on his dignity, carrying a brief case.

"I trust you have some explanation, Chief Superintendent . . ."

Maigret had disliked Maître Leloup on sight. Now, he

fell upon him as if he were a dear friend whom he had not seen for twenty years.

"The telegram? Why didn't he address it to me direct? Come on! Come on! Hand it over!"

"Here it is, but I doubt if you'll be able to make anything of it, and I'm not sure I ought to let you have it, unless you are prepared to tell me more."

Maigret snatched the telegram out of his hand.

Inform Chief Superintendent Maigret portrait photograph only present received from late aunt (Stop) Dismantled frame on off-chance (Stop) Found concealed letter somewhat cryptic but in my opinion highly damaging to third party (Stop) Situation regarding succession completely altered since Joseph Boynet's death not due to natural causes and murderer and accomplice cannot inherit (Stop) Desirous of doing my duty but without prejudice (Stop) Arriving Paris tonight (Stop) Etienne Monfils

"Don't you think my client . . . ?" ventured the lawyer.

"Your client is the hero of the house, Maître Leloup. He raises a point that I hadn't even thought of. Once it is established that Joseph Boynet was murdered by his wife and her lover, she is retrospectively dispossessed of his fortune, which reverts to the Boynets and the Machepieds."

"But . . ."

The Chief Superintendent was no longer listening. He stood motionless in the middle of the vast corridor of police headquarters, within sight of the door of his own office. Close by was the glass-walled waiting room in which, one foggy morning . . .

A child was in process of being born somewhere or other, little dreaming that the fees for his delivery would be paid by a small band of gentlemen whose fingers were adorned with flashy rings. . . . And they, for their part, were no doubt engaged, at this hour, in the complexities of a game of *belote* at Chez Albert on Rue Blanche.

And what of Monsieur Charles, closeted with his lawyer under the discreet eye of the benign Torrence? What was he thinking?

"Not a bad idea!"

He was startled by the sound of his own voice, and he was not alone in this. Spencer Oats and Maître Leloup, taken unawares, nearly jumped out of their skins.

"I was thinking of that dodge with the photograph," he explained apologetically.

"The old woman sized up her cousin pretty accurately. She understood provincial life. . . . Well, gentlemen, back to work."

And, with a little snort, he embarked upon the interrogation of all those who had visited police headquarters on the morning of the murder.

He finished with the last of them, a small-time pimp, at one o'clock in the morning. In conclusion, dropping his burned-out cigarette on the floor, the man said:

"Well, there it is! I try to do someone a favor, and I land myself in the soup. . . . What's the best I can hope for, Chief Superintendent? Two years?"

Madame Maigret had already been on the telephone three times.

"Hello! . . . No! . . . Don't wait for me . . . I'll probably be home pretty late!"

Suddenly, he had a craving for a plate of *choucroute garnie*, in a brasserie in Montmartre or Montparnasse, in company with his American.

Afterward, they saw one another home, and weaving from bar to bar and from beer to beer, they drank the night away. After all, it was only fair that Spencer Oats should have something to talk about when he got back to Philadelphia.

All the same, if it had not occurred to Monfils to take the photograph out of its frame . . .